Winter will be over soon, and so are these ~~titles~~
guaranteed to put a spring in your step! Lose yourself
in an absorbing read from Harlequin Presents....

Travel to sophisticated European locations and meet
sexy foreign men. In *The Greek's Chosen Wife* by
Lynne Graham, see what happens when gorgeous
Greek Nikolas Angelis decides to make his convenient
marriage real. *The Mancini Marriage Bargain* by
Trish Morey is the conclusion of her exciting duet,
THE ARRANGED BRIDES—we brought you the first
book, *Stolen by the Sheikh,* last month.

Fly to more distant lands for Sandra Marton's UNCUT
story, *The Desert Virgin.* Feel the heat as ruthless
troubleshooter Cameron Knight rescues innocent
ballerina Leanna DeMarco. If you haven't read an
UNCUT story before, watch out—they're almost
too hot to handle!

If you like strong men, you'll love our new miniseries
RUTHLESS. This month in *The Billionaire Boss's
Forbidden Mistress* by Miranda Lee, a boss expects
his new receptionist to fall at his feet, and is surprised
to find she's more of a challenge than he thought.
Lucy Monroe's latest story, *Wedding Vow of Revenge,*
promises scenes of searing passion and a gorgeous hero.

The Royal Marriage by Fiona Hood-Stewart is a classic
tale of a young woman who has been promised in
marriage to a royal prince. Only she's determined
not to be ruled by him and her declaration of
independence begins in the bedroom!

We hope you enjoy reading this month's selection.
Look out for brand-new books next month!

Harlequin Presents®

UNCUT

Even more passion for your reading pleasure!

Escape into a world of intense passion and
scorching romance! You'll find the drama, the
emotion, the international settings and the happy
endings that you've always loved in Harlequin
Presents® books. But we've turned up the
thermostat just a little, so that the relationships
really sizzle…. Careful, they're almost
too hot to handle!

Look for some of your favorite bestselling
authors coming soon in

UNCUT!

This month's UNCUT story sees the first
in Sandra Marton's gripping new trilogy
THE KNIGHT BROTHERS. Don't miss Matthew's and
Alexander's stories, coming soon in May and July!

Coming in May 2006:
Captive in His Bed
by Sandra Marton
#2537

Sandra Marton

The Desert Virgin

uNcut

HARLEQUIN®

TORONTO • NEW YORK • LONDON
AMSTERDAM • PARIS • SYDNEY • HAMBURG
STOCKHOLM • ATHENS • TOKYO • MILAN • MADRID
PRAGUE • WARSAW • BUDAPEST • AUCKLAND

ISBN 0-373-12525-9

THE DESERT VIRGIN

First North American Publication 2006.

All about the author...
Sandra Marton

SANDRA MARTON wrote her first novel while she was still in elementary school. Her doting parents told her she'd be a writer someday and Sandra believed them. In high school and college, she wrote dark poetry nobody but her boyfriend understood, though looking back, she suspects he was just being kind. As a wife and mother, she wrote murky short stories in what little spare time she could manage, but not even her boyfriend-turned-husband could pretend to understand those. Sandra tried her hand at other things, among them teaching and serving on the board of education in her hometown, but the dream of becoming a writer was always in her heart.

At last Sandra realized she wanted to write books about what all women hope to find: love with that one special man; love that's rich with fire and passion; love that lasts forever. She wrote a novel, her very first, and sold it to the Harlequin Presents line. Since then, she's written more than sixty books, all of them featuring sexy, gorgeous, larger-than-life heroes. She's a four-time RITA® award finalist. From *Romantic Times BOOKclub* she's received five awards for Best Harlequin Presents of the Year and a Career Achievement Award for Series Romance.

Sandra lives with her very own sexy, gorgeous, larger-than-life hero in a sun-filled house on a quiet country lane in the northeastern United States.

"Sandra Marton introduces sexy, action-adventures to Presents with *The Desert Virgin*. This story is one nonstop exhilarating ride as an irresistible alpha hero rescues the woman, who will become his true love, and saves them both as they traverse a desert nation to gain their freedom.... Sandra Marton has once again outdone herself and has raised the bar of excellence in romance."

—Shannon Short, *Romantic Times BOOKclub*

CHAPTER ONE

AT THIRTY-TWO, Cameron Knight stood six foot four inches tall. He had green eyes and a leanly muscled body, courtesy of his Anglo father; jet-black hair and knife-sharp cheekbones, thanks to his half-Comanche mother. He loved beautiful women, fast cars and danger.

In all the ways that mattered, he was still the dangerously handsome bad-boy half the girls in Dallas, Texas, had lusted after when he was seventeen.

The only thing that had changed was that Cam had turned his passion for danger into a career, first in Special Forces, then in the Agency, and now in the firm he'd started with his brothers.

Knight, Knight and Knight had made him rich as hell. Men on three continents asked for his help when things got out of hand.

Now, to Cam's surprise, so had his father.

Even more surprising, Cam had agreed to give it.

That was why he was flying high over the Atlantic in a small private jet, heading for a dot on the map called Baslaam.

Cam checked his watch. Half an hour to touchdown. Good. Things had happened so fast that he'd had to spend most of the flight reading his father's files on Baslaam. Now, he had time to try to relax.

A man about to drop into an unknown situation needed to be ready for anything. Deep breathing exercises, what one of his instructors at the Agency had always referred to as tai chi of the mind, did the job.

Cam put back his leather seat, closed his eyes and let his mind drift. Maybe because he was on a mission for his father, he thought about his life. What he'd made of it. What he hadn't.

How close he'd come to meeting his father's bitter predictions.

"You're worthless," Avery used to tell him when he was a kid. "You'll never amount to anything."

Cam had to admit he'd seemed determined to prove his father right.

He'd cut school. Gotten drunk. Smoked dope, though not for long. He didn't like the loss of self-control that came with the short-lived high.

By seventeen, he was a kid heading for trouble.

Angry at his mother for dying, at his old man for caring more for money than for his wife or sons, he'd been a time bomb ready to go off.

Late one night, driving a winding back road, watching the speedometer needle of his souped-up truck climb over one hundred, he'd realized he was going past the dark house of a cop who'd roughed him up a year back. It hadn't been much, just a little hard handling.

What mattered was that the cop had done it as a courtesy to Cam's father.

"His old man wanted me to give the kid somethin' to think about," Cam had heard the cop tell his partner.

With those words echoing in his head, Cam had pulled his truck to the side of the road. Climbed a tree, jimmied open a window, stood over the sleeping cop while the bastard snored, then went out the same way he'd gone in.

It was an exhilarating experience. So exhilarating that he did it again and again, breaking into the homes of men who danced to his old man's tune, taking nothing from the break-ins but the satisfaction of success.

One night, it all came apart. He was in college by then, home for a long weekend…and he'd come within a whisper of getting caught.

Playing dangerous games was one thing; being stupid was another. Cam quit school, joined the Army, got recruited into Special Forces. When the Agency expressed interest, he said yes. Risk was what you ate and breathed in covert operations.

He thought he'd found a home.

Not true. It turned out the Agency sometimes asked things of you that made you a stranger, even to yourself.

His brothers had taken similar routes. Fast cars, beautiful women, playing Russian roulette with trouble, seemed the path a Knight took to manhood.

A year apart in age, they attended the same college on football scholarships. They'd even all scored touchdowns in the same game, one memorable championship season.

They'd all quit school after a couple of years, joined the Army, then Special Forces and, finally, maybe inevitably, the clandestine labyrinth of the Agency.

Just as inevitably, they'd grown disillusioned with what they found there.

The brothers returned to Dallas and went into business together. Knight, Knight and Knight: Risk Management Specialists. Cam had come up with the name after hours of solemn planning and not-so-solemn drinking.

"But what in hell does it mean?" Matt had asked.

"It means we're gonna make ourselves a fortune," Alex had said, grinning.

And they did. Powerful clients paid them exorbitant amounts of money to do things that would have made most men's bellies knot with fear.

Things that the law just wouldn't—or maybe couldn't—handle.

The only person who seemed oblivious to their success was their father…and then, last night, Avery had turned up at Cam's Turtle Creek triplex.

Avery hadn't wasted time on preliminaries. He'd explained that his oil contracts negotiator in the sultanate of Baslaam hadn't reported in for almost a week and was unreachable by cell phone or satellite computer.

Cam had listened, expressionless. Eventually Avery fell silent. Cam still said nothing, though by then he knew what had brought his father to him.

Moments crawled by. Avery grew red-faced. "Goddammit to hell, Cameron, you know what I'm asking."

"Sorry, Father," Cam said tonelessly. "You'll have to tell me."

For a second, Cam figured Avery was going to walk out. Instead, he took a deep breath.

"I want you to fly to Baslaam and see what the hell's going on. Whatever your fee is, I'll double it."

Cam had tucked his hands in the pockets of his trousers, leaned back against the railing of the wraparound terrace that looked out on the city.

"I don't want your money," he said quietly.

"Then what do you want?"

I want you to beg, Cam had thought. But the damnable code of honor drummed into him by the Army, by Special Forces, by the Agency and maybe even by his own convictions, kept him from saying the words.

This was his father. His blood.

Which was why, less than eighteen hours later, he deplaned into a desert heat so fierce it slammed into him like a fist.

A small man in a white suit hurried toward him.

"Welcome to Baslaam, Mr. Knight. I am Salah Adair, the sultan's personal aide."

"Mr. Adair. Good to meet you." Cam waited a couple of seconds, then made a show of looking around. "Isn't the rep from Knight Industries with you?"

"Ah." Adair smiled brightly. "He has undertaken a survey beyond the Blue Mountains. Did he not notify you of his plans?"

Cam returned the bright smile. The negotiator was an attorney. He wouldn't have recognized signs of oil from signs for a neighborhood gas station.

"I'm sure he notified my father. He must have forgotten to tell me."

Adair led him to a black limo, part of a mixed convoy of old Jeeps and new Hummers. All the vehicles held soldiers bristling with weapons.

"The sultan sent an escort in your honor," Adair said smoothly.

The hell it was. No escort would involve so many

armed men. And where were all the regular citizens of Baslaam? The paved road that led into town was empty. As the only road in a country trying to claw its way into a semblance of the twenty-first century, it should have been crowded with traffic.

"The sultan has arranged a feast," Adair said with an oily smile. "You will taste many delicacies, Mr. Knight. Of the palate…and of the flesh."

"Great," Cam said, repressing a shudder. This part of the world, delicacies of the palate could make a man's stomach roll. As for delicacies of the flesh…he preferred to choose his own bed-mates, not have them chosen for him.

Something was wrong in Baslaam. Very wrong, and dangerous as hell. He had to keep alert. That meant no strange foods. No booze. No women.

Definitely, no women.

Where were all the women?

Leanna wasn't sure exactly how long she'd been locked in this all but airless, filthy cell. Two days, maybe two and a half—and in all that time, she'd yet to see a female face.

She kept hoping she would because a woman would surely listen to her. Help her escape from this hellhole.

That was right, wasn't it?

It had to be.

Leanna eyed what little water remained in the bucket she'd been given that morning. If she drank it, would they give her more? Her throat was parched from the heat, though the worst of it was over. She had no watch—the men who'd kidnapped her had torn it from her wrist—but the blazing eye of the sun had begun its descent behind the mountains. She knew because the shadows in her squalid prison were growing longer.

That was the good news.

The bad was that the darkness would bring out the centipedes and the spiders. Dinner plates with legs, was what they were.

Leanna closed her eyes, took a deep breath, told herself not to think ahead. There were worse things than centipedes and spiders waiting for her tonight. One of her guards spoke just enough English to have told her so. Remembering the way he'd laughed still made her shudder.

Tonight, she would be taken to the man who'd bought her. The king or chief or whatever he was called of this horrible place. The bugs, the heat, the taunts of her captors would all seem like pleasant memories.

"The Great Asaad will have you tonight," the guard had said, and his gap-toothed grin and obscene hand gesture had guaranteed she understood exactly what that meant.

Leanna began to shake. Quickly she wrapped her arms around herself, willed the trembling to stop. Showing her fear would be a huge mistake. It was just that it was hard to imagine how this could have happened. One minute she'd been rehearsing *Swan Lake* with the rest of the *corps* on the stage of a tired but beautiful old theater in Ankara. The next, she'd stepped out a side door for a break, been grabbed and tossed in the back of a stinking van…

The door swung open. Two enormous men, their hands the size of hams, stepped into the cell. One stabbed his thumb upright in the air and mumbled something she assumed meant she was to go with them.

She wanted to fall to the floor. She wanted to scream. Instead, she stood tall and glared at her captors. Whatever came next, she'd face it with as much courage as she could manage.

"Where are you taking me?"

She could see that she'd surprised them. Why not? She'd surprised herself.

"You will come."

The giant's English was guttural but clear. Leanna put her hands on her hips.

"The hell I will!"

The men lumbered toward her. When they clamped their meaty paws around her arms, she dug her heels into the vermin-infested straw that covered the floor but it didn't do much good. They simply lifted her to her toes and dragged her between them.

Still, she fought. They were strong but so was she. Years spent *en pointe* and at the barre had toughened her muscles. She had a terrific high kick, too. It had once earned her a spot in a Las Vegas chorus line and she put it to good use now.

She got the Talking Giant right where he lived.

He doubled over in pain. His partner found that vastly amusing but before Leanna could give him the same treatment, he twisted her arm high behind her back, jammed his ugly face into hers and snarled something she couldn't understand.

She didn't have to. Between the stink of his breath and the spray of his spittle, the message was clear.

Still, why would that stop her? She knew what came

next. Talking Giant had told her this morning, though she'd already suspected. Two other girls from the troupe had been kidnapped with her. One, same as Leanna, had assumed they'd been taken for ransom but the other had quickly eliminated that possibility.

"They're slavers," she'd whispered in horror. "They're going to sell us."

Slave traders? In this century? Leanna would have laughed, but the girl added that she'd seen a news report on the white slave trade on television.

"But who would they sell us to?" the first girl said.

"To any son of a bitch who can afford to buy us," the third girl had answered, her voice trembling. Then she'd added details, enough so the first girl had tossed her cookies.

Leanna had never been the type to throw up or swoon. Ballerinas looked like fairy-tale princesses on stage but the truth was, dancing was a tough life, especially if you came to it via a publicly funded dance program instead of some expensive Manhattan studio.

While one girl vomited and the other shivered, she'd fought the ropes that bound her. But their captors burst in, held them down and injected something into their arms. She'd come to in this horrid cell, alone, knowing she'd been sold…

Knowing it was only a matter of time before her owner claimed her.

Now, that time had come.

The giants dragged her down a long corridor that stank of sweat and human misery. They shoved her into a small room with stained concrete walls and a drain in the middle of the floor, and slammed the door behind her. She heard the sound of a bolt sliding into place but she threw herself at the door anyway, pounding it with her fists until her knuckles hurt.

Then she slumped to the cold floor, looked at the stained walls, at the drain. At the dark, wet stain around it.

She buried her face in her hands.

A long time later, she heard the bolt sliding open. Leanna began to tremble.

"No," she whispered to herself, "don't let them see how scared you are." Somehow, she knew that would only make things worse. Slowly she dragged herself to her feet and lifted her chin.

A woman entered the room. Leanna sagged with relief. Two men with cold, dead eyes stood behind her but the woman's bearing made it clear she was in charge.

"Do you speak English?" Leanna asked. No reply, but that didn't prove anything. "I hope you do," she said, trying to sound reasonable instead of terrified, "because there's been an awful mis—"

"You will disrobe."

"You *do* speak English! Oh, I'm so—"

"Leave your clothing on the floor."

"Listen, please! I'm a dancer. I don't know what you think I—"

"Do it quickly, or these men will do it for you."

"Do you hear me? I'm a dancer! And I'm an American citizen. My embassy—"

"There is no embassy in Baslaam. My lord does not recognize your country."

"Well, he'd better. Otherwise—otherwise—" The woman jerked her head toward the men behind her. Leanna shrieked as one of them moved faster than she'd have thought he could and grabbed the neck of her T-shirt. "Stop it! Take your hands off—"

The shirt tore to the hem. Leanna lashed out but he laughed and caught her wrists in one hand, lifting her off her feet so the other man could yank off her sneakers and her cotton trousers.

When she was stripped to her bra and panties, they flung her to the floor. Leanna scrambled toward the wall and screwed her eyes shut. Maybe she was dreaming. She *had* to be dreaming.

This couldn't be real, couldn't be real, couldn't be—

She shrieked as a gusher of warm water hit her in the face. Her eyes flew open. A scraggly line of serving-women surrounded her. Some held steaming pitchers, some held soap and towels. The men had dragged in an enormous wooden vessel…

A tub?

"Take off your undergarments," the woman in charge snapped. "Bathe yourself well. If you are not clean enough, you will be punished. My lord, the sultan Asaad, will not tolerate filth."

Leanna blinked. She was in an improvised bathroom. That was the reason for the drain in the floor.

A bubble of hysterical laughter rose in her throat.

The ruler of this godforsaken place had bought her, had her thrown into a vermin-infested hole in the ground. He was going to make her into his newest sex toy.

But first, she had to scrub behind her ears.

Suddenly everything that had happened, that was happening, seemed unbelievable. Leanna let the laughter out. Peals of it. The servant women stared at her in disbelief. One giggled and slapped her hand over her mouth, but not quickly enough. The woman in charge slapped the one who'd dared laugh, barked an order, then rounded on Leanna in rage.

"Perhaps you would like to appear before my lord beaten black and blue!"

Leanna looked her tormentor in the eye. She was tired of being afraid, tired of behaving like a whipped dog. Besides, all things considered, what could she possibly lose?

"Perhaps *you'd* like to appear before him and explain how you managed to damage the merchandise."

The woman blanched. Leanna's heart was racing but she smiled coolly.

"Tell your goons to get lost and I'll get into that tub."

Stalemate, but only for a few seconds. Then the woman snarled a command and the men marched out of the room.

Leanna took off her bra and panties, stepped into the tub, eased down in the hot water and let it soothe her body while her brain worked feverishly to come up with an escape plan.

Unfortunately, by the time she was pronounced clean enough for the sultan of Baslaam, she still hadn't thought of anything. Improvisation was for actors, not for classically-trained dancers.

But she'd never been a coward.

If she had to, she'd die proving it.

CHAPTER TWO

CAM had seen a lot of places in upheaval.

Baslaam wasn't in upheaval. It was in collapse. It didn't take training as a spy to see that.

No people. No vehicles. A gray sky, filled with plumes of smoke. And the vultures, scores of them, circling overhead.

Things were not going well in the sultanate, he thought grimly.

Adair offered no explanations. Cam, nobody's fool, didn't request any. All he kept thinking was that the pistol he'd secreted in his briefcase might end up being useful.

The sultan was waiting for him in a marble hall with ceilings easily twenty feet high. He sat on a gold throne elevated on a silver platform, and he sure as hell wasn't the man Avery had described.

The sultan, his father had told him, was in his eighties. Small. Wiry. Hard-eyed and determined.

The man on the throne was in his forties. He was big. Huge, really, a mass of muscle just starting to turn to fat. The only resemblance between the picture Avery had painted and this behemoth were the eyes, but the hardness in them spoke more of cruelty than determination.

Had there been a coup? That would explain a lot of things, including the disappearance of his father's representative. It was a good guess the poor bastard was one of the unlucky souls attracting the attention of the vultures.

Cam had only one real question. Why hadn't he been disposed of, too? The man on the throne must want something of him. What? He had to find out, and do it without giving away the game.

Adair made the introductions. "Excellency, this is Mr. Cameron Knight. Mr. Knight, this is our beloved sultan, Abdul Asaad."

"Good afternoon, Mr. Knight."

"Excellency." Cam smiled politely. "I expected you to be older."

"Ah, yes. You thought you would meet my uncle. Unfortunately, Uncle passed away most unexpectedly a week ago."

"You have my sympathy."

"Thank you. We all miss him. I had similar expectations about you, Mr. Knight. I thought the man who owns Knight Oil would be much older."

"My father owns the company. I'm his emissary."

"Indeed. And what brings you to our humble nation?"

"My father thought the sultan—I should say he thought that *you*," Cam said, with a polite smile, "might prefer to discuss the final details of the contract with me instead of his usual negotiator."

"And why would I wish that?"

Why, indeed? "Because I have his full authority. I can come to agreement on his behalf." Cam offered a just-between-us smile. "No middleman, as it were, to slow the process."

The sultan nodded. "An excellent suggestion. As it is, your predecessor and I have had some areas of disagreement. He wanted to make changes in the wording your father and I had already agreed upon."

Bull, Cam thought coldly, but he smiled again. "In that case, it's a good thing I've come, Excellency."

"I am sure Adair explained that the gentleman in question has gone to visit the plains beyond the Blue Mountains."

"He mentioned it."

"It was my suggestion. I thought it might do him good to get away from the city for a while. Take a break, I think you would call it. The plains are very beautiful, this time of year."

The lie bore no resemblance to what Adair had said, and ended any last hope that his father's representative might still be alive. The desire to leap onto the platform and grab the sultan by the throat was fierce.

Cam forced a polite smile. "A fine idea. I'm sure he's enjoying himself."

"Oh, I can promise that he's getting a good rest."

The son of a bitch grinned from ear to ear at the double entendre. Once more, Cam fought back the desire to go for him. Outnumbered, he'd be dead before he got within ten feet.

"While he rests," Asaad said, "you and I can finalize things." The sultan clapped his hands. Adair hurried forward with a pen and a sheaf of papers that Cam instantly recognized. "All it takes is your signature, Mr. Knight. So, if you would be so kind…?"

Bingo. This was why the negotiator was dead—and

why Cam was still alive. Asaad needed a signature on the dotted line to move forward with the deal.

"Of course," Cam said smoothly. "First, though, I'd like to get some rest. It was a long journey."

"Signing a document is not difficult."

"You're right, it isn't—which is why, surely, it can wait until tomorrow."

Asaad's eyes narrowed but his tone remained smooth. "In that case, permit me to ease the stress of your journey. I have arranged a small celebration of welcome."

"I appreciate the gesture, sir, but really—"

"Surely you will not disappoint me by turning down my hospitality."

The sultan's smile didn't reach his eyes. Was the so-called celebration part of a plan to lure Cam into compliance, or was it for more sinister reasons? Either way, Cam was trapped. The sultan had planned a party. There was no way out.

"Mr. Knight? What do you say? Will you be my guest?"

Cam inclined his head. "Thank you, Excellency. I would be delighted."

Three hours later, the festivities were finally drawing to a close.

The evening had started with a feast. Platters of grilled meats, sweets, pastries...and bowls of other things, easily identified and grotesque, eaten by custom in decades long past.

The first time such a course appeared, Cam felt his stomach roll. He managed a polite smile, began to shake his head—and realized that a hush had fallen over the several dozen armed men seated at the long table.

Every eye was on him.

The sultan raised his eyebrows.

"This is a great delicacy, Mr. Knight—but we will understand if you are not prepared to partake of it. Not all men can be like the men of Baslaam."

Hell. Was this going to be a pissing contest? A Baslaamic version of "I'm tougher than you are"? If so, Cam couldn't afford to lose. He smiled, leaned forward and scooped a ladleful of the quivering mess on his plate.

"A delicacy, Excellency? In that case, I can't pass it up."

He ate quickly, tasting slime and something even worse on his tongue, keeping his gut from rebelling by reminding himself that he'd eaten things as bad in other places. A soldier in the field couldn't be choosy. Bugs, lizards, snakes… Protein, he told himself, that's all this was.

There was a perceptible murmur when he swallowed the last of the stuff. Cam smiled. Asaad didn't smile back. His expression was ugly. The bastard had lost the first round and he didn't like it.

"Delicious," Cam said politely.

Asaad clapped his hands. A servant scurried in, carrying an oversize urn. "Since you enjoyed that so much, perhaps you would like to sample another of our delicacies. A drink, made from… Well, I won't tell you the ingredients but I assure you, it is more potent than anything you've had before." At his nod, the servant filled two cups with a brown liquid. Asaad took one, handed Cam the other. "Unless, of course, you'd rather not?"

It *was* a pissing contest. Juvenile, even pathetic, but what choice did he have except to accept the challenge?

Any show of weakness and he could end up keeping his father's rep company. Asaad needed his signature but there were ways to get it that didn't involve pretending they were all one big, happy family.

"Mr. Knight?"

"Excellency," Cam said, lifting the cup to his lips. The liquid smelled like rotting fish but he'd survived worse one long night in Belarus, when he'd downed endless shots of homemade vodka in a face-off with a thickheaded guerilla leader. He held his breath, tossed his head back and drank the swill in one gulp.

"Great stuff," he said calmly, and held out his empty cup. Another murmur of approval filled the great hall. Asaad's face grew dark as a thundercloud.

"Do you ride horses, Mr. Knight?"

Maybe the sultan was thickheaded, too. Asking a born-and-bred Texan if he rode horses was like asking a pigeon if it could fly.

"Some," Cam said politely.

Moments later they were outside in a vast courtyard lit by torches, racing over the hardpacked sand on the backs of half-wild ponies in a game that involved sticks as thick as baseball bats, a leather ball and a looped rope hanging from a tree. Cam had no idea what the rules were but he stayed on his snorting mount, managed not to get clobbered by men wielding their bats with abandon, and whacked the ball straight through the loop.

The sultan's men cheered. Asaad's face turned purple. He shouted for silence.

"You are a worthy opponent," he said in a voice that made clear the statement was a lie, "and I shall reward you."

With what? A knife across the throat? A bullet in the head? Lose the game and you were dead. Win, and you were dead, too. Asaad was a psychopath, and capable of anything.

Cam's muscles tensed and he fought to keep his tone calm.

"Thank you, Excellency, but the only reward I want is—"

The words caught in his throat. Two of the sultan's men were coming toward them. They were big, bigger than the sultan...

Twice as big as the woman they all but dragged between them.

The first thing he noticed was that her hands were bound.

The second was that she was naked. No. Not naked. It was just that her skin was the palest gold and what little she wore was only a shade darker.

Gold cupped her full breasts; a gold thong rode low on her flat belly. A thin gold chain adorned her narrow waist; slender, twisted ribbons of gold hung from the chain and swayed sinuously with each thrust of her long legs.

Her feet were encased in golden sandals, the heels so spiked they could have been declared lethal weapons. Tiny bells dangled from the straps of the sandals and tinkled softly at her every step. Her hair was gold, too, and tumbled forward in silken disarray around her downcast face.

"Do you like your reward, Mr. Knight?"

"She is..." Damn it! Cam cleared his throat. He hadn't expected anything like this golden creature and it had thrown him. The sultan knew it; he could hear it in the bastard's oily voice. "She is an amazing sight, Excellency."

"Indeed." Asaad smiled. "I will have her brought closer, yes?"

The obvious answer was no. This woman was a trap. It didn't take a genius to know that. Cam had been wined and dined; he'd been entertained with a crazy game of desert polo. Asaad had softened him up and now he was moving in for the kill. An hour with this *houri* and he'd sign the contract, no questions asked. He'd be too sated to do anything else.

At least, that was what Asaad figured.

And, damn, it was tempting. Cam could imagine what it would be like to spear his hands into that spill of hair, raise the woman's face so that he could see if it was as perfect as the rest of her. He could imagine tasting her breasts, stripping away that gold thong…

"Mr. Knight?"

Cam shrugged as if getting a better look at the woman didn't matter.

"As you wish, Excellency."

The sultan snapped his fingers. The men dragged the woman forward. When they were a few feet away, she raised her head and looked straight at Cam.

His breath caught in his throat.

She had wide-set eyes the color of the Mediterranean, fringed by incongruously dark lashes. A small, straight nose. A delicate chin and a mouth—God, what a mouth! It was meant for things men dreamed of in the dark hours of the night.

Cam felt himself turn hard as stone, his erection so

swift and powerful that he had to shift his weight to ease the discomfort of it.

Asaad barked an order. The guards shoved the woman forward the final few feet. She stumbled, then regained her footing. One of the men snarled a word and she obeyed what must have been an order to bow her head again.

"Well, Mr. Knight?" Asaad's voice was a purr. "What do you think?" Smiling, he stepped closer to the woman, caught a handful of her hair and jerked her head up. "Is she not exquisite?"

"She is—she is very beautiful."

"Yes. She is. She has spirit, too. A magnificent creature, yes?"

What was she? A woman from the harem? But her hands were bound. Why?

"She is, Excellency." Cam paused. He didn't want to sound too curious. If he did, Asaad would probably stretch out whatever game they were now playing. "Is she a prisoner?"

The sultan sighed. "Yes. Unfortunate, don't you agree? What you can see of her is beautiful." Asaad slid his meaty hand down the woman's throat, over her breast, cupped first one mound of flesh and then the other. When she tried to jerk away, his fingers clamped around her wrist. "But her soul is ugly."

Cam looked at the sultan's meaty fingers, biting into the woman's flesh.

"It's difficult to imagine that a woman like this—any woman, for that matter—could do something so terrible it would anger a man like you, Excellency," he said, hoping the barbarous lie would work.

It seemed to. Asaad's grip loosened.

"You are correct, Mr. Knight. I am a kind man. A generous one. But Layla pushed me beyond human endurance."

The name suited the setting. So did her costume. But the blue eyes and golden hair threw him. They were rare in this place. Hell, they were all but unknown.

"I imagine you are thinking she is not from here."

Right on the nose, you greasy bastard. Cam smiled lazily, as if it were something that really wasn't of much interest. "I did wonder, yeah."

"I bought her," the sultan said matter-of-factly. "Oh, not the way it sounds, I assure you. We are an ancient culture, sir, but we abhor slavery. No, the lady came to me willingly. She is a dancer. That is what she prefers to call herself but really, she is… I think your word is whore."

Cam nodded. He understood. He'd been in this part of the world before. Women like this called themselves models, actresses, dancers…but Asaad was right. Basically they were whores for sale to the highest bidder.

The blonde stood straight and tall under his scrutiny. Was she trembling? Maybe, but the wind blowing in from the desert was cool and she was damned near naked. That could explain it. So could the fact that she was Asaad's prisoner. From what he'd seen of things, that would make anybody tremble.

Asaad leaned closer. "I met her on holiday in Cairo. She was performing in a club. I sent her a note… Well, surely you know how these things go." He dug his elbow into Cam's ribs, as if buying a whore's favors was something they had in common. "Layla is a woman of, shall we say, significant talent. That is why, when it came time to return home, I offered to take her with me."

Cam shot another look at the woman. Her head had come up; she was staring almost blindly into the darkness beyond the courtyard and yes, she was definitely trembling.

Not that it meant a damn to him.

"And she accepted," he said, making it a statement instead of a question.

"Of course. She knew it would be worth her while. All went well for a few weeks. She was inventive. Imaginative." Asaad gave a deep sigh. "But I wearied of her. A man needs variety, is that not so?"

"Wouldn't sending her back to Egypt be simpler than making her your prisoner, Excellency?"

The sultan threw back his head and laughed. "You are an amusing man, Mr. Knight. Yes, of course. Much simpler. And that was what I attempted to do. I made arrangements to send her home—with a substantial bonus." His smile faded. "Yesterday, just before she was to leave, I learned she'd stolen a priceless jewel from my chambers. This, after all I'd given her! When I confronted her, she tried to put a dagger between my ribs." Asaad let go of Cam's elbow and stepped back. "I have been trying to decide what to do with her."

What to do? *How* to do it, the sultan surely meant. The penalty for theft and attempted murder could only be death. That the woman had survived a day was something of a miracle. Tomorrow, she'd be food for the vultures. But tonight...

And then Cam understood. Asaad had a plan, and it was as transparent as glass.

The woman was shaking, she was on display—but she was docile. Why? If her life was at stake, why wasn't she pleading for mercy?

There could only be one reason. The sultan must have promised her mercy. All she had to do to was follow his orders, and those orders surely involved Cam.

She was to be a gift.

He'd take her to bed, she'd perform tricks that would keep him from thinking and Asaad would let her live. But why? Was she supposed to put a knife in Cam's belly while she feigned passion? No. Asaad would want him alive until he signed the contract.

Maybe the son of a bitch just wanted to watch through a hole in the wall. Maybe his men were going to break in and grab him while he was screwing the woman.

Maybe that was the night's real entertainment.

"Don't look so grim, Mr. Knight. Layla tried to kill me. She doesn't warrant your concern."

"Frankly, Excellency," Cam said with a man-to-man grin, "my only concern—if you want to call it that—is over the world's loss of the lady's considerable talents."

"Indeed." The sultan leaned toward him. "Then you will be happy to hear that I have decided to give her to you for the night."

"You are most generous," Cam said, trying to look as if he meant it. "But you may recall what I said earlier. I've had a long day, and I am—"

"Tired." Asaad winked. "But we are both warriors, and a warrior knows the best way to renew his strength. Unless… Is she not to your liking? She has the morals of a desert viper but you have nothing to fear. My men will stand guard outside your door."

Cam almost laughed. He'd just bet they would.

"She will give you pleasure beyond your wildest dreams."

"I'm certain she would, Excellency. Still—"

"Take a better look, Mr. Knight."

Asaad cupped the woman's breast and pinched the nipple through the gold fabric. She flinched but made no sound. Cam jammed his hands into his pockets to keep from grabbing the sultan by the throat. So what if Asaad manhandled her? She was his to do with as he pleased.

He'd seen worse in his years undercover. Black ops wasn't for the faint of heart.

Still, something about what was happening made his belly knot.

"Touch her yourself, Mr. Knight. See how smooth her skin is."

Asaad ran his hand over the woman, from her breasts to her belly. She swallowed hard, her throat visibly constricting, and drew a breath that made her nipples press against the gold cloth that contained them.

The sultan laughed.

And Cam felt his body respond.

He wanted to touch her. Shove Asaad out of the way and put his hands on Layla instead. He despised himself for it but the need burned in his belly, hot as flame.

He wanted to bare her breasts, see if her nipples were the pink of rose petals or the pale rust of apricots. Taste them, roll them on his tongue while he slid his hand between her thighs, under the thong to the hot, wet center of her.

He told himself there was a logical reason for this insanity. All the adrenaline he'd burned these last hours, anticipating danger, meeting it, being on constant guard…

Any man would be more than ready for the release you found in sex. Never mind that the woman was a whore, a thief and worse. That she'd sold herself to God only knew how many men.

She was beautiful, and he wanted her…but he wouldn't take her. She was a golden trap.

Cam stepped back, drove every X-rated image from his head.

"Do what you want with her," he said coldly. "I'm not interested."

There was a silence. Then the woman's head came up. Her lips curved in an insolent smile as her eyes swept over him, lingered on the taut fabric at his groin, then rose to his face.

"What he means, Lord Asaad," she said softly, her eyes never leaving Cam's, "is that he's not man enough to use me properly."

She spoke in English but the insult was clear. A collective roar went up from the assembled men. After a shocked moment, the sultan threw back his head and shouted with laughter.

The world went black, narrowed down to only the woman's taunting smile and the contempt on the face of the sultan.

Cam growled an obscenity, pushed past him, curled his hand around the narrow band that joined the golden cups of the woman's bra and ripped it in half.

Her face went white. She threw up her bound hands in a frantic attempt to cover herself but Cam grabbed her wrists and pulled her hands down.

Now, the only sound in the vast courtyard was the rasp of his breath.

"You like to play rough?" he said softly. His mouth twisted in a cold smile. Slowly, purposefully, he let his eyes sweep over her.

Her breasts were perfect. Round and high, just the size to fill his palms. The tips, beaded by the rapidly chilling night breeze, were the shade of ripe apricots.

"Very nice," he said in a voice he barely recognized as his own.

Eyes locked to hers, he lifted his hand, ran his knuckles lightly over her breasts. When she tried to jerk away, her guards grabbed her arms and forced her to stand still as Cam stroked her nipples, warm silk against his fingertips.

"I've changed my mind," he said thickly. "I'll take her."

Her scream was lost in the delighted howl of the crowd as he scooped her up, tossed her over his shoulder and headed for the palace.

CHAPTER THREE

THE laughing crowd of barbarians parted like the Red Sea as the American strode through it.

Leanna had come up with a plan, but it had all gone wrong.

A hand reached out, fondled her bottom. She shrieked. The pig who'd touched her said something that made the others laugh even harder.

"Please," she gasped to her captor, "please, you've got this all wrong."

He grunted and shifted her weight. For all she knew, he couldn't even hear her. She was hanging over his shoulder like a bag of laundry, bound hands clutching desperately at the ragged ends of her bra.

As if modesty mattered at a time like this.

As if anything mattered, except forcing this man to listen.

A couple of hours back, it had all seemed so clear. What she'd do, how she'd do it. The giants had brought her to the sultan who'd looked her over and smiled as if she were a mouse in the paws of a cat.

"Very nice," he'd said softly.

Then he'd told her that he'd have to put off their first

time together, as if, dear God, as if being raped by him was something to look forward to.

"I have a guest," he'd said, "an American business associate. Take him to bed, keep him occupied so that he hears and sees only you. I will reward you by having you taken to the airport and sent home."

And Santa and the Easter Bunny were kissing cousins.

Asaad would never set her free, but Leanna had decided that seeming to go along with things was her best bet.

She'd be brought to the American's room like a gift-wrapped package. The door would shut, he'd smile at his luck and she'd say, very softly because the walls surely had ears, *Thank God you've come. I'm an American, I was kidnapped. I'm supposed to keep you busy so that you're deaf and blind to whatever the sultan is planning to do to you. We have to get out of this horrible place before that happens.*

Instead she'd been delivered like a package, in front of the sultan. Okay, she'd thought. She'd wait until she and the American were alone.

It had never occurred to her he'd refuse Asaad's gift.

The man's eyes had glinted with desire when he saw her. His body had quickened. It had been impossible not to notice.

And then his hot stare had turned to ice. She had no idea why. She'd had to do something, and fast.

The way he looked—the hard face and muscled body, the stubble on his jaw, the faded jeans and leather boots—were almost overtly masculine. This was a man who wouldn't take an insult lightly.

So she'd deliberately taunted him. That was the good news.

The bad was that it had worked too well. He'd ripped her bra in half, handled her with an icy lust that terrified her more than anything that had happened yet…

But it wasn't too late. He was her countryman.

That had to count for something.

The guards at the palace doors snickered as he marched past them. The doors swung shut and she and the American were alone.

Now, she told herself, and took a breath. Despite everything, she knew she had to stay calm. Sound rational. If she did, surely, she could get through to him.

"Mr. Knight? That's your name, isn't it?"

The American began climbing the stairs.

"Mr. Knight. The sultan lied. I didn't steal anything. I didn't try to kill him. I'm not even named Layla."

She knew he could hear her. There was no crowd, no noise, only the sound of his boot heels hitting the marble floor as he made his way down a corridor.

Why didn't he say something?

"Did you hear me?" Still no answer. "Mister. Answer me. Say something. Tell me you understood what I—"

"Shut up."

Leanna shrieked and pounded her fists against his back. It was about as effective as pelting a stone wall with pebbles.

"Damn you," she screamed, and sank her teeth into his shoulder. All she got for her effort was a mouthful of denim shirt, but it got his attention.

"Do that again," he snarled, "and I'll reciprocate."

"You have to listen! I know what Asaad told you, but—"

"You want to be gagged as well as tied?"

Oh God! He was as much a savage as the sultan. How stupid she'd been to think his nationality and hers would create a bridge of decency in this godforsaken place.

She heard another snicker of laughter, saw another pair of grinning soldiers. He brushed past them and stepped through a set of massive doors and into an enormous room.

A room dominated by a bed the size of a stage.

He dumped her on it, walked to the doors and shot the brass bolts.

"Alone at last," he said coldly.

Leanna scrambled back against the headboard. "Mr. Knight," she said desperately, "I know what you think…"

He gave a low, dangerous laugh. "I'll bet you do."

"But you're wrong. I'm not… I'm not what the sultan…" Her eyes widened as he began unbuttoning his shirt. "Wait. Please. You don't—you don't understand."

His gaze dropped to her breasts, all but spilling from the torn bra she clutched like a lifeline.

"Let go of it."

"What?"

"Let go of that thing." He looked up, his smile icy enough to freeze the marrow of her bones. "I like what I saw in the courtyard, Layla. I want to see it again."

"My name isn't Layla. It's—"

"I don't give a damn what your name is. We're not going to have wine and exchange phone numbers. We're going straight to the main event." His voice roughened. "Let go of the bra."

"I'm not a—a whore," she said desperately. "I'm not anything Asaad said I was."

Knight's face turned hard. "No games, baby. You think I'm in the mood to play the barbarian and the virgin, I'll tell you right now that I'm not."

"I'm not playing anything. I'm just trying to—"

"How do you want to do this?

"I don't—I don't follow the…"

"The easy way?" His tone softened, turned to raw silk. "You want, I can make this good for you."

"I don't want you to make this anything for me! I keep telling you, I'm an American, just like you."

"You're not anything like me." He bared his teeth in a chilling grin. "If you were, I wouldn't want you in my bed."

"Give me a minute. Just one minute. I can explain everything. Asaad said things about me, but—"

"But they aren't true."

"Yes!" Her voice rose in excitement. "Oh, thank God! You *do* understand! You—you… What are you doing?"

It was an unnecessary question. What he was doing was horrifyingly obvious.

He was getting undressed. Toeing off his boots. Shrugging off his shirt, letting it fall to the floor.

Leanna's heart jammed in her throat.

She'd felt his strength when he carried her but seeing him like this, his chest exposed, his shoulders bare, she knew she had no chance against him. The man who owned her for the night was as sleek as a panther, and just as deadly.

He'd said he wasn't in the mood for games but he was playing a game of his own, letting her babble and beg for mercy. Maybe it amused him. All she could be certain of was that when he tired of it, he'd overpower her without any effort at all.

"I know you're angry at me, but—"

"I'm not anything at you, Layla, except tired of hearing you talk."

"What I said to you down there, what I said to you… I just wanted to get your attention."

"Yeah. Well, you got it."

"I had to find a way to be alone with you."

"I'm touched."

His hands were at his belt, undoing the buckle. At his fly, opening the button above the zipper, revealing the start of a line of silky hair that arrowed down, down, down…

Terror skittered through her like a small animal clawing for escape but she knew better than to let it show. That might excite him even more.

"I need your help. I swear it! Just hear me out and—"

"You haven't answered my question." He started toward her, his gaze moving over her breasts, her belly, her thighs. "I can take you slowly. Or I can take you without any preliminaries. It's your call."

Leanna choked back a sob as he reached the bed. She tried to roll away but he grabbed her ankle and pulled her into the center of the mattress.

"The hard way," he growled. "That's fine with me."

"No," she panted, and gave up any attempt at reason. He was on her now and she fought for her life, kicking, bucking, kicking again, aiming for his groin, catching him in the gut with her knee instead.

"Okay," he said grimly, "that's it."

His hands were quick and hard as he undid the rope around her wrists, then dragged her arms over her head and bound them to the headboard. When she kicked harder, he whipped the belt from his jeans and wound it around her right ankle, securing it to a footpost before rolling from the bed and returning with a scarf, a tie, something bright and silky that he looped around her left ankle and tied to the other footpost.

Terror swooped down on her, smothering her in feathery black wings. She opened her mouth and her scream, shrill and high, pierced the air.

"Scream," he said. "That's fine with me. You can damned well bet we've got a crowd listening at the door. You scream, you'll liven up the show."

"Don't," she whispered, because a whisper was all she was capable of now, "please, don't, don't, don't."

"Why not?" he said coldly. "Because I haven't got the price of admission?"

He came down on the bed beside her. "Oh God," Leanna said. She turned her face away, closed her eyes and let the tears come.

All she could do now was survive.

She was good, Cam thought. He had to give her that.

It was one hell of a performance. From sexy temptress to terrified innocent in, what, twenty minutes? Unfortunately the routine was about as real as Asaad's offer of her as a gift.

Why the big act? The tease, then the turnoff.

The only certainty was that the lady was a fine actress. She was probably an even better lay. How many men had paid for her favors? He let his gaze move slowly over her as she lay spread-eagled before him, those glorious breasts bare to his eyes, her golden thighs spread for his pleasure.

His erection, already hard enough to hurt, was going to kill him if he didn't get inside her soon.

So, why was he hesitating? Her fear wasn't real. It was part of the performance. That was fine with him. He'd done a lot of things in bed that had nothing to do with the missionary position. Silk scarves could be a turn-on.

Besides, she'd given him no choice. The kind of game she was playing had only one possible conclusion.

It was a game, wasn't it?

Was it possible she was telling the truth? That she didn't want him to screw her? No. Impossible. If that were the case, she could have had her wish without any effort. He'd already told the sultan he didn't want her.

Why deliberately taunt him unless she wanted to make him change his mind?

Cam's eyes narrowed.

The whole thing smelled like a scam. Her being dragged in like a criminal, Asaad saying he was going to have her killed, the lady's aren't-you-man-enough routine followed by her implausible plea for help.

Had everything that happened been meant to heighten an erotically charged situation so that the stupid American would think with his hormones instead of his head?

If so, it had worked.

But he'd calmed down. He was thinking again. And what he thought was that the door was bolted. The windows, too. He'd taken care of that before his meeting with the sultan. He had a Beretta stashed beneath the mattress and a beautiful woman in his bed.

His body tightened.

And he was going to have her.

Stress always took its toll. Life in Special Forces and then in the Agency had taught him that. Meditation had its place but there were times you needed more than that.

Some men used alcohol, others used drugs. Cam had learned, a long time back, that what worked for him was hot, raw sex. Sex with a woman beautiful and experienced enough to make you forget the niceties of civilized behavior.

Layla damned well fit the bill.

Some long minutes inside her, feeling her honeyed heat, tasting that soft-looking mouth, and he'd be fine. He'd be better when she stopped playacting and admitted she wanted it as much as he did. She was good, pretending she didn't, but she'd slipped a few minutes ago when he was taking off his shirt.

What he'd seen in her eyes then wasn't panic. It was awareness of him as a man.

And that was how he wanted it, now that he was back in control of his emotions. A woman who liked sex was the only kind worth screwing.

Games? Sure. A gorgeous woman, his for the taking but pretending she wasn't, could be a turn-on.

Rape wasn't.

It was time for the act to end and the real thing to start.

Cam looked down again at the woman lying beneath him. She was beautiful, a creature of pale gold skin and darker gold hair. She was a dancer, Asaad had said. Never mind the rest. That was how he'd think of her now, as his partner in an erotic dance they'd both enjoy.

"Look at me," he said. When she didn't, he caught

her chin in his hand and forced her face to his. "Open your eyes."

Slowly, she did as he'd commanded. Her irises, ringed in black, were the deep blue of a summer sky. Her lashes were long and thick, spiky with tears. Tears? Definitely, she was good at what she did. At making a man want her and, God, he wanted her with every beat of his blood.

"I've never paid for a woman," he said huskily, "but if I did, I might just start with you."

He reached out, traced the fullness of her bottom lip with the tip of his finger, felt her tremble. He bent toward her, brushed his mouth over hers.

"All the time we were in the courtyard," he whispered, "I kept thinking about your mouth. About all the things it was made to do."

Slowly he put his lips to hers again, harder this time, hard enough to feel the swift intake of her breath.

"Stop pretending you don't want this," he said roughly. "Kiss me. Let me taste you. Let me do this right."

She made a little sound and tried to pull away as he lowered his head to hers again, and he thrust his hand into her hair, felt the golden curls twine around his fingers as he held her mouth captive to his.

The game was still on.

He kissed her. Her mouth was warm and soft. Cam groaned, changed the angle of the kiss until she made a little sound and her lips parted.

"That's it," he said and slid his tongue into her mouth, felt the sweet delicacy of her shudder as he tasted her.

God, she was driving him crazy.

The feel of her mouth. The smell of her skin. The press of her naked breasts against his chest…

He drew back, cupped the small, perfect mounds. Her eyes flew open; color flooded her face.

"You have incredible breasts," he said hoarsely.

"Please," she whispered, "please, I beg you…"

"What?" He watched her eyes as he feathered his thumb against one nipple, saw the black pupils all but swallow the blue irises, heard the catch of her breath.

"Do you like that? Tell me. Tell me what you like."

He bent to her, licked her nipple. She moaned and he bent to her again, blew lightly against the pearled flesh, then sucked it into his mouth.

It was like touching a lighted match to dry kindling.

She arched toward him and a sob burst from her throat, the sound high and wild and filled with something he couldn't quite define.

Could it be wonder?

He wanted it to be, he thought fiercely. Wanted to be the first man who'd wrung that sound from this woman who had lain in God only knew how many other men's arms.

She was breathing raggedly, moaning softly, writhing against his hand as he caressed her. Stroked her nipples. Kissed her warm flesh. She said something he couldn't hear, whispered it as he touched her.

"Tell me," he said, his voice urgent with need. "Tell me what I make you feel."

Cam slipped his hand between their bodies. Slid it up her leg. Felt the heat of her skin. His nostrils flared at the sudden, unmistakable scent of her desire.

"God," she whispered, "God…"

She raised her head from the pillows. Sighed and offered him her mouth.

With a fierce growl, he took the kiss she'd offered. Sank into it. Felt the first, tentative touch of her tongue against his, heard her sigh and knew he was taking her with him into a dark velvet whirlpool of desire where nothing and no one mattered except this.

He felt her starting to tremble against him.

Stop, a voice deep within him whispered. *This is a mistake. For God's sake, man, stop!*

But it was too late. He was aching, as much for her final surrender as for his own release.

She moved against him, a little roll of her hips that made him groan. This—making love to her, feeling her swift response and knowing that the restraints still tied around her wrists and ankles left her exquisitely open and completely vulnerable to him—was incredibly exciting.

But he wanted more.

He wanted her arms around his neck, her legs around his hips as he poured himself into her.

Cam ran his hand higher, heard her swift intake of breath when he reached her thigh. Her skin was hot. Burning, as he was burning. He kissed her throat, heard her make that little sound women make when they stand balanced on the brink of forever in a man's embrace.

"Tell me now," he said. "What you like. What you want. I'll make it happen, I promise."

"Untie me," she whispered, "and I'll show you."

He hesitated, but just for a heartbeat. Then he undid the rope around her wrists, shuddered when she ran her hands down his arms to his chest. He kissed her and she nipped lightly at his lip.

"Please," she said, her breath mingling with his.

His hesitation lasted a little longer this time. But the beautiful witch in his arms moved against him with the delicacy of a cat and he stopped thinking, leaned back and quickly freed the restraints from her ankles. Then he came down to her again, kissed her again, slowly, slowly, using his tongue as he would use his erection inside her in another minute because he couldn't wait much longer.

He'd take her once, hard and quick, then slowly, so that it lasted a long, long time.

She shifted her weight again, the faintest easing of her hips. He looked down into her face. Her eyes glittered.

"You said you'd show me what you want," he whispered.

"Yes," she said, "I will."

Later, thinking back, he knew he'd heard something in those simple words that should have given it all away but right then—hell, right then, he was a man only capable of following the aroused compass of his own flesh.

"Show me," he said, and then he went absolutely still at the feel of cold steel against his belly.

He inhaled sharply, instinct making him try to press his gut against his backbone, but the kiss of the steel went with him.

The woman in his arms smiled. Then she put her lips to his ear.

"I've got a knife pressed to your belly," she said in a voice as soft as a lover's caress. "You make a stupid move, Mr. Knight, I swear I'll use it."

CHAPTER FOUR

His reaction was everything she'd hoped for.

Pocketing the little nail file had been sheer good luck. She'd snatched it when she was being dressed for her meeting with the sultan, slipped it down her thong for the moment she could use it, and now that moment had come.

When Knight sucked in his belly, as if he could somehow put distance between himself and the sharp tip, she almost wept with joy. This was the first thing that had gone right.

She'd made one bad decision after another, underestimating Asaad, underestimating his horrid visitor...

And underestimating her reaction to what had just gone on in this bed.

Knight had tied her down. Touched her. Kissed her. She'd fought, struggled, done everything she could to keep him off her...

And then—and then, something had changed. Her terror had been lost in a rising tide of heat. His hands on her breasts, his taste on her mouth...

Never mind all that.

The tables were turned. She had a weapon and its

sharp tip was right where she wanted it. The balance of power had changed. And it was damned well going to stay that way.

When she felt him start to shift his weight, Leanna countered by putting a little more pressure on the file.

"Don't do anything stupid," she whispered.

"What the hell do you think you're doing?"

His voice was soft. She knew he was keeping it down so anybody with an ear pressed to the door wouldn't grow suspicious.

"I'm pressing the point of a very sharp knife to your stomach, Mr. Knight. Don't give me reason to use it."

"Just take it easy, okay? Stay nice and calm and tell me what you want me to do."

"I want you to get off me."

"Sure. No problem. You just— Hey! Take it easy with that blade."

"Don't try to buy me off, Mr. Knight. I want you off me, and then I want you to get me out of this place."

"Fine. Give me the knife and we'll talk about it."

She almost laughed. Did he think she was stupid? Do what he'd asked and he'd tie her up before she had time to blink. Then he'd punish her for what she'd done. His powerful body would press her down into the mattress. He'd kiss her until she whimpered for mercy…until her treacherous body melted under his touch as it had before.

Anger at him, at herself, at the fact that nothing made sense, turned her voice cold.

"There's nothing to talk about. Do what I want or I'll slide this blade right between your ribs."

"Is this the knife you tried to use on Asaad?"

"Exactly."

"I thought you told me you didn't try to kill him."

"I lied."

"Why? What's the sense in—"

Leanna poked the tip of the file against his belly. "Remember what you said about having a conversation, Mr. Knight? I'd keep that in mind, if I were you. No wine, no cheese, no explanations. I'm the one giving orders now."

"Then try giving one that gets me off you. It's difficult to think while you have that thing in my gut…and while you're lying under me."

Leanna felt her face flood with heat. He was right about the lying under him part. They were still pressed together like lovers—and as impossible as it seemed, he was still aroused, that hard ridge of his masculinity taut against her belly.

"Besides, if we don't start doing something pretty soon, we'll have a roomful of people demanding their money back."

She blinked up at him. "What?"

His voice was whisper-soft, as if he were saying the things a man might say to a woman in bed.

"Don't tell me you didn't figure we'd have an audience."

"You mean…watching?"

"Maybe. But they're certainly listening." A wolfish smile curved his lips. "How else will Asaad know when to make his move?"

It was her turn to be surprised. "You know he's going to do something to you?"

"I figured as much, yeah."

"Well, if you figured it, you must have an idea."

A smart man would have but for the last half hour or so, Cam knew he'd been anything but smart. Still, he had the Beretta within hand's reach.

And she had a knife at his gut.

"I do," he said confidently.

"What is it?"

"You get that knife out of the way. Then I'll tell you my plan."

"Forget it." She hesitated. "Isn't there someplace we can talk without worrying about people hearing us?"

"Maybe."

"Where?"

"The bathroom. It's got marble walls and floors. We go in, close the door, turn on the water to drown out the sound of our voices and there's a chance we can have maybe a five minute conversation before they get nervous."

"If you're right—if we're being watched—won't they wonder if we go into the bathroom together? It could only be so we can get away from them."

"Not if we play our cards right."

"What do you mean?"

"I mean, I'm going to make a thing out of wanting to bathe you."

The tip of the blade skidded against his belly.

"You use that thing, our chance of getting away goes from one to zero." Cam eased back, his eyes never leaving hers. "You know what I want?" he said, his voice suddenly loud in the quiet of the room. "A bath. Scented oil, candles…"

She stared at him.

"Say something," he hissed.

"A—a bath? That sounds—it sounds—"

"Yeah. It does."

Cam scooped her from the bed, held his breath and waited for the kiss of whatever it was she had in her hand, a carving knife, a steak knife—except, how big could it be if she'd been able to hide it in the bit of gold string she called a thong?

"Bath time," he said loudly as he carried her across the floor, into the bathroom and elbowed the door shut behind him.

She started to speak. He put his finger over her lips and waited. Nothing happened. No pounding at the bedroom door, no shouts, no footsteps rushing down the hall. Still holding her, he reached for the taps in the tub and turned them on.

Water drummed loudly against the marble.

"Now," he said quietly, "give me that knife."

"Tell me your plan. Then we'll see about the knife."

Cam clenched his jaw. The lady was tough as well as beautiful. He'd have to handle her with a little more caution.

"I'm going to put you down. Just don't do anything you'll regret."

"You'll have more to regret than I will."

Carefully he set her on her feet. The knife had disappeared—for the moment, anyway.

"Okay," he said, "tell me what you know."

"Asaad is planning something."

"And?"

"I'm supposed to distract you."

"That's it?"

"Isn't it enough?"

Cam ran his hand through his hair. "Great," he muttered. "My own Salome."

"What?"

"Salome. Remember? The babe who got a guy so hot he didn't even know it when she whacked off his head for the king."

"While you're being clever, Asaad's probably getting ready to kill us both. What are we going to do about it?"

We? He almost laughed. There was no "we." All he was interested in, when it came to this lady, was getting that weapon—whatever it was—out of the hand she was keeping behind her back. Then he'd say *adios* to her and get the hell out.

She was on her own. If he took her with him, she'd be a liability.

"Okay," Cam said, lying through his teeth. "But you aren't going to like my plan."

"Try me."

"They're waiting for the big moment. The climax, as it were."

Color striped her cheeks. "You think this is funny?" She moved closer to him and he felt the quick kiss of steel against his belly again. "Maybe you think this is funny, too."

"What I think," he said lazily, "is that you talk too much."

He pushed her back against the wall, cupped her face in one hand and kissed her. She gasped in surprise and when she did, he angled his mouth over hers and took the kiss deeper. She made a little sound and he reminded himself it was all an act.

All an act, he thought…and pressed his thumb

against a pressure point between her collarbone and her throat.

She went limp in his arms. The weapon she'd threatened him with fell into his waiting hand. Not a carving knife. Not a steak knife. Not a knife at all, Cam thought wryly. It was a nail file, maybe three inches long.

He raised his eyes to her face. The color was slowly coming back, washing her skin with the palest pink.

"What—what did you do to me?" she whispered.

He smiled tightly. "A little trick, that's all."

"Bastard!"

"Oh, right. You're not into tricks, baby. You're into the truth… Like that routine in bed. The moaning. The sighing. All real, right?"

Crazy as it was, he half-waited for her to say yes. Yes, it had been real, not an act…

"I did what I had to do."

"Remember those words," he said, and that was when Leanna knew he was going to escape without her.

She couldn't let that happen. There had to be a way to make him agree to take her along, but what was it?

"Okay," he said softly. "Here's how we're going to do this. You stay here. I'll go back into the bedroom and—"

"No."

"What do you mean, no?"

"We stay together."

"This is the only way."

Damned right, it was. His gun was in the bedroom, and his boots, and so was a window that opened onto a path that led to the courtyard.

"Why should I wait here if you're going into the other room?"

"I have a gun in the other room. I have to get it."

"You're planning on going out one of the bedroom windows."

"Don't be crazy."

Leanna jerked her chin toward a large window near the tub. "What about that?"

"What about it?"

"Does it open?"

"Of course it opens." Well, it probably did. He'd tried the windows in the bedroom, not this one, but what did it matter? He wouldn't be using it.

"Show me."

"I told you, my gun—"

"You're lying. There is no gun. You just want to escape away without me."

"Why would I want to do that?"

Her smile was sweet. "Look," she said. "The water's almost at the top of the tub."

"Yeah. Fine." Cam turned off the taps. "Okay. I'm going to open this door and—"

"You're going to open the window," she said, and let out a blood-curdling scream.

Cam's eyes widened in disbelief. He cursed, slapped his hand over her mouth, but it was too late. Something smashed against the doors in the other room.

He spun around, threw the bolt on the bathroom door. It was old and it wouldn't hold up to more than a few blows, but any delaying action was better than none.

Salome was already at the window, pushing at the lock. "It's jammed!"

Cam cursed, shoved her aside, beat at the lock with his fist. The nail file. Would it…? Yes. A couple of jabs and the lock sprang open.

The sounds from outside the other room grew louder. The doors would give way any second.

"They're coming," she said in a panicked whisper. "They're coming!"

"What a surprise," Cam muttered as he ripped the shutters away, kicked out the glass and hoisted himself onto the wide sill.

"Please! Don't leave me behind!"

He jerked around, looked down at the woman, saw her golden hair streaming over her naked breasts, saw her sky-blue eyes filled with hope and terror. She'd gotten herself into this mess, come to this hellhole for whatever she could get from Asaad, and now she'd forced him into making his escape unprepared. The Beretta that might be his only chance at survival was as much beyond his reach as the world he'd left behind when he left Dallas.

"Please," she whispered, "don't leave me."

The sounds from outside the bedroom grew louder, as if the door were being pounded with a battering ram.

"Please," she said desperately.

With a muffled curse, Cam leaned toward her. "You give me a minute's trouble and so help me, I'll dump you. You got that?"

"Yes. Yes, yes, yes!"

He held out his hand. She grabbed his wrist and he yanked her onto the sill beside him.

"We're going to jump," he said, "and hit the ground running."

"Run where?"

"Wherever I tell you. Ready?"

She nodded. "Ready."

He could hear her teeth chattering. She was scared to death. Good, he thought grimly. Scared, she just might be tractable.

"One," he said. "Two…"

He laced his fingers through hers. They jumped and she landed on her feet, despite the sky-high heels.

Cam took a quick look around. They were in a walled passageway; overhead, a thin slice of lemon-yellow moon cast a cold glow over the hardpacked earth where, hours before, he'd first set eyes on Salome.

"Are you as good at running as you are at playing games in bed, Salome?" He didn't expect an answer, nor did he intend to wait for one. Instead, he shoved her behind him. "Follow me," he said. "Run as if the hounds of hell were on your heels."

He was fast. He could do five miles without breaking a sweat. If she could keep up, fine. If not…

He skidded to a stop when they reached the edge of the wall. She banged into him. He motioned her to stay back, then peered around the corner.

The vehicles that had made up the convoy were still parked in the driveway.

"Stay here," he whispered.

"No way."

"Stay here, damn it!" He grabbed her hand, shoved the little file into it. "Use this if you have to."

He started out from the shadows.

"Wait!" she whispered, her voice urgent.

He swung back and looked at her. "What?"

"I don't know your name. I mean, I can't keep calling you Mr. Knight."

"It's Cameron. Cam."

"Cam," she said, and gave him a wobbly smile.

Impulsively he plunged his hand into her hair, cupped her head and kissed her. Then he took a deep breath, crouched low and started running toward the parked vehicles.

Luck was with him. The drivers had never removed the ignition keys. He plucked them from each vehicle and shoved them in his pocket. He'd just reached the Humvee at the head of the line when the throaty growl of an angry mob broke the silence of the night.

The sultan's goon squad had beaten down the door and found nobody home.

Cam swung around. "Salome," he yelled. "Run!"

She hurtled toward him, threw herself into the Hummer as he turned the key. The engine roared to life and the vehicle shot forward just as the first of Asaad's men came flying around the corner.

"Get down," Cam snapped. When she didn't move fast enough, he reached over, palmed the top of her head and shoved her down in her seat. "Damn it, what did I say? You do as I tell you."

"I dropped the nail file," she said breathlessly.

"Tough," he snarled, as he shifted gears. "I guess you'll just have to rough it."

He knew damned well she'd been thinking of the file as a weapon lost but they had bigger worries now, thanks to her. She'd forced him into an escape he hadn't planned and wasn't ready for.

The chatter of a Kalashnikov shattered the night but

they were moving fast. Before very long, the men and the bullets were too far back to matter.

Ahead lay the endless desert.

And whatever slim hope they had of survival.

CHAPTER FIVE

THE Humvee flew across the hardpacked sand.

Cam tossed all the keys he'd taken out the window while Leanna fumbled with what was left of her bra. Somehow, she managed to tie the ends together. It was surreal enough to be racing across the desert next to a man like Cameron Knight without doing it with her breasts bared.

Had she really been dancing in Ankara a few days ago, practicing pliés and arabesques? Now she was in a place ruled by psychopaths, her life in the hands of a cold-eyed stranger who drove the Hummer as if it were a race car, his eyes fixed on whatever was ahead.

Sand, she thought bitterly. That's what was ahead. Sand and her life, in this man's hard hands.

His hands hadn't felt hard when they'd touched her. Her skin—her skin still tingled from his touch.

Heat swept into her face and she swung toward the side window. Why think about it? She was a trained dancer. She knew how to get into a role. That was what she'd done, in his arms, and without conscious effort.

Now she had another role to play. She had to keep him from dumping her by being—

"…useful."

Leanna blinked. "What?"

"I said, how about doing something useful?"

"Like what?"

Like finding a way to cover yourself up, Cam thought. His hands tightened on the wheel. At least she'd managed to rig the bra so her breasts were covered, but they still threatened to spill from those glittering gold cups. Her legs, stretched out before her and highlighted by the snaking ribbons of gold, had to be a thousand miles long. And if that damned thong rode any lower on her belly…

"See what you can find to take with us after we ditch the Hummer."

"Why would we ditch it?"

"Because it's too easy a target to spot."

Leanna popped open a compartment and rummaged through it. "We've got a notepad and a pen."

"Sure to come in handy for souvenir postcards to the folks back home. Anything else?"

"Matches. And some sticky stuff that smells pretty good."

"Show me."

She held out a cream-colored lump. Cam nodded.

"Halvah. Candy. High in protein, high in fat. A good find. Anything else?"

"This little box. Some kind of electronic gadget."

A flicker of light reflected in the mirror caught Cam's attention. He watched it for a couple of seconds. Headlights, but a long way back. Asaad's men had found them, but they still had a little time.

Salome's gaze followed his. "Is that—is it Asaad?"

"Don't worry about it. Let me see that gadget." Cam took his eyes from the windshield for a quick look. "It's a GPS. A global positioning device. Assuming it's still got juice, we'll be able to tell where we are."

"And then what?"

"And then I can give the coordinates to some people who can help us."

"How?"

"I have a cell phone."

"A cell phone? Then, why don't you—"

"I did. I tried earlier today but I couldn't get a signal."

She sat back and folded her arms over her breasts. No, not *over* them, exactly. It was more like *under* them so the gold cups lifted, made an offering of the golden skin whose honeyed essence he could still taste on his tongue.

"Damn it," Cam said, furious at her, at himself, at the stupidity of thinking about sex at a time like this, "don't just sit there. Climb in the back. See what else you can find. You need to put on some clothes."

"I'm fine."

"Yeah, well, I'm not. It's cold in the desert at night. You go into shock, you'll slow me down. Get in the back and come up with something."

She gave him a look he figured might not be friendly but she got up on her knees and peered into the back of the Hummer.

It was an unfortunate move. It put her derrière within easy reach. Cam locked his eyes on the windshield. Her hip brushed his shoulder. A couple of the gold ribbons trailed across his thigh and he had a sudden image of how those ribbons would drape over his lap as he pulled her down onto him.

He kept this up, he was going to drive the freaking Hummer straight into a sand dune.

"I found something!"

So had he, but what good would it do him in a moving car? "What?"

"A rucksack. There's stuff in it. Water. A shirt. A T-shirt. And—"

"And what?"

"And, uh, and nothing. I thought there was something but... Nope. That's it."

The hell it was. She was lying, but why?

"Great. Keep the shirt, toss me the T."

She climbed back over the seat. Her thigh brushed him again. He thought of how he'd put his hand between her legs, felt the silky heat of her skin...

The Humvee swerved.

"Did you see something?"

Damned right, he'd seen something. His inability to get this all in perspective. But he understood the problem. Sexual frustration. He'd been moments from taking what he wanted, what Salome was so good at promising but not delivering, and he'd been interrupted.

What he needed, he thought coldly, was completion. That all too famous, twenty-first century word. Closure. And he'd have it—assuming he could lose the vehicles on their trail. He'd take Salome in his arms, lay her down in the sand, tear aside that damned thong and ride her until they were both exhausted.

Then he could concentrate on saving his skin and, by coincidence, hers.

"Hang on to the steering wheel."

She leaned across him. Her hair brushed his cheek

and he drew the clean scent of it deep into his lungs. Quickly he pulled the T-shirt over his head.

"Okay," he said brusquely. "You can sit back."

"You didn't answer me, Cameron. Did you see something? Because I think—"

"It's Cam," he said sharply. "And do me a favor, okay? Don't think. I don't want you to tax yourself. Just put that damned shirt on and dump the rest of the stuff you found into the pack."

Leanna glared at Cameron. At Cam. She wouldn't make that mistake again.

She pulled on the shirt, gave a little shudder and burrowed into the soft cotton. Much, much better. Not only was she warmer, she didn't have to watch him give her looks that said she was some kind of X-rated video queen.

This man, she thought coldly, was the meanest-tempered SOB she'd ever met. Okay, maybe she'd pushed things a little, made him take off without his gun, but without her help, he might be dead.

Or they might still be in bed, she on her back and he—and he—

Leanna drew the pack closer. The feel of it was pure comfort.

Last time she'd carried a pack, she was a twelve-year-old Girl Scout. It had held a canteen, a bag of Trail Mix and a peanut butter sandwich.

Now, the pack in her arms held water and halvah and matches and a GPS…

And a gun.

An automatic. Anybody who went to the movies or watched TV would know that much. It was all she knew, but it was enough. She wasn't defenseless anymore.

She glanced at Cam. Coldhearted bastard that he was, she had to admit he was also a gorgeous hunk of masculinity.

So what? Good looks didn't change a thing. She didn't trust him as far as she could throw him—which wouldn't be far, considering how he was built.

She'd felt his full weight when she'd been pinned under him on the bed.

All of him, so powerful and hard.

All of her, so feminine and soft.

And when he'd put his hand between her legs…if she'd moved, just a little. Raised her hips. Opened her thighs. If she'd moved, and he'd moved…

"They're behind us."

Leanna peered out the back and saw a string of lights. Her heart lurched.

"Can't we go faster?"

"I've already got my foot to the floor."

"What can we do?"

"We need a diversion."

"What diversion?"

"I'm trying to see what's out there."

"Sand is what's out here," she said, trying to sound nonchalant.

"I can make out the outline of something. Rocks. A hill. If I can send the goons behind us away from it, we might have a chance."

Leanna clutched the knapsack closer. She could feel the outline of the gun. Maybe now was the time to tell him about it. Maybe she could trust him. Maybe…

Cam swung the Hummer swung hard to the right. "Open your door."

"Open my door?"

"Isn't that what I said?"

She stared at him, then did as he'd ordered.

"Good. Now take a deep breath and jump out."

"Jump out?"

"Stop repeating everything, damn it. I'm going to slow down. The second I do, you jump. Try for some distance. Roll. Do it properly and you won't get hurt."

Her heart began to race. She'd figured him right. He was stone-cold. He'd decided to save himself by giving her to Asaad.

Leanna pulled the gun from the pack. It felt heavy as lead in her hand but she forced it up and aimed it squarely at him.

"Keep driving."

He looked at her and did a double-take. "Where'd that come from?"

"Never mind." Her voice was shaky. So was her hand. "I swear, I'll shoot you unless you put your foot on the gas and get us out of here."

"Salome." Cam's voice was low and very calm. "Give me the gun."

"I'm going to count to three. You hear me? One. Two…"

"Look out!"

It was the oldest trick in the world but it worked. Leanna swung around to confront the supposed danger behind her. The Hummer swerved drunkenly as Cam grabbed her wrist and applied enough pressure to make her cry out.

The gun tumbled from her suddenly nerveless fingers.

"No," she yelled, "no, you son of a bitch! You can't do this to—"

"Remember to roll," he said, and shoved her out into the night.

Instantly he jerked the wheel hard to the left, increased his speed and looked in the mirror. As he'd hoped, the sultan's men stayed right on his ass.

It was a trick he'd used before, but never with a woman.

He'd done the best he could. Slowed the car. Told Salome how to manage the fall. If she let instinct take over, she'd be okay.

That bit with the gun… He knew she'd found something, but a gun? He'd never figured on that. And then to pull it on him…

Cam took a last look in the mirror. If he drove too far, he'd never find her when he backtracked. It was tempting. Let her get out of this mess on her own…

A long incline was coming up. Just what he needed to make this work.

He eased his foot off the gas, waited until the Hummer was almost at the top of the incline. Then opened his door and dove out, landing shoulder-first, rolling as far as he could before he rose up in a crouch.

The Hummer was sailing down the far side of the slope, headed for points unknown. He flattened against the sand as the pursuit vehicles roared past, then winced as he got to his feet. His shoulder hurt but it would be no more than a bruise. Quickly he checked that the gun was still tucked into his waistband. Then he hoisted the pack over his arm and got moving.

All he had to do now was follow his tire tracks and find Salome.

Except, it wasn't happening. Where the hell was she?

"Salome?"

Nothing. Only the increasing wail of the wind.

"Salome! Where are—"

She sprang on him out of the darkness, hissing and clawing like a tigress. The pack fell to the ground as she tried to rake his cheek; her knee would have connected with his groin if he hadn't been fast enough.

"Hey! Take it easy! It's me."

All that earned him was a punch that slipped inside his upraised hands and bounced off his jaw before she danced away from him, then came at him again. Okay, he thought grimly, so be it.

She was quick but she didn't know the first thing about fighting. He feinted left, knowing she'd follow. When she did, he caught her, wrapped her tightly in his arms and hoisted her off her feet.

"Damn it, woman, are you nuts?"

"I'm nuts, all right," she panted, "for thinking you'd help me."

He thought about telling her he'd never offered to help her but sanity prevailed. Now wasn't the time for logic.

"Calm down!"

"Calm down? Calm down? You threw me out of a moving car!"

"I slowed to a crawl. If you'd jumped when I did, you'd probably have a couple of broken bones."

"You wanted to get rid of me!"

"Then, why'd I come back to find you?"

"You didn't. You just—you just stumbled across me."

Cam snorted. "That can't make sense, even to you."

Leanna twisted against him. "Let go!"

"With pleasure. Just remember, you slug me again, I'll—"

"You'll what? Tie me up? Throw me over your shoulder? You already did all that, remember? What kind of man are you?"

Cam put her on her feet. "The kind who doesn't have to put up with this crap," he said with brutal candor. "You might want to keep that in mind."

Leanna stared at him. Even in these ridiculous heels, he towered over her. She already knew how strong he was. Now, she knew that he'd do whatever it took to save himself from being captured.

Okay. And maybe to save her.

The wind caught at her hair and tossed it in her eyes. She lifted a shaking hand to push it away.

Had he really come back for her? It was possible. Okay, it was more than possible. Still, all she knew for sure was that he was a man who'd make love to a woman who begged him not to.

She had begged, hadn't she? Begged him to stop. Of course she had. Those things she'd felt when he'd fondled her breasts, when he'd slipped his tongue into her mouth...

"You have a face like an open book, Salome."

His voice was sexy and rough. Her eyes flashed to his. Did he know what she'd been thinking?

Leanna drew herself up. "In that case, you know that if you try any more tricks, I'll—"

"What?" His eyes narrowed. "Stab me? Shoot me?" He cupped her shoulders, lifted her to her toes. "What other little toys have you got stashed?"

"Stashed?" She looked down at herself, the oversize shirt hanging open over her skimpy costume, and gave a harsh laugh. "You have to be kidding."

"I ought to strip-search you."

She felt heat rise in her face. "I told you, I haven't got—"

"Yeah. So you say." His gaze moved over her slowly, insolently, all but peeling the clothes from her body. "I'm going to pat you down, Salome. Just stand still, take it nice and easy and it'll be over real quick."

"No! I will not let you—" She caught her breath as he ran his hands down her arms. "Damn you, stop that! What do you think you're—"

His hands slid under the shirt. Lifted to her breasts. His eyes locked to hers as he cupped them, feathered his fingers over the soft curves and over her nipples. His expression was coolly detached but she could see a tiny muscle beating high in his cheek.

To her horror, she felt her nipples tighten.

"Don't," she said, trying to grab his wrists. "You have no right…"

His hand slid over her belly.

Oh God! A quick, damp heat bloomed between her thighs.

"Stop it! I don't—" Her voice shook. "I don't have any hidden weapons."

The hell she didn't, Cam thought, and slipped his hand between her thighs and cupped her.

Her entire body went rigid. His already was. He could feel the heat of her burning his palm. Could a woman fake that? Could she tremble at a man's touch unless she meant it? Could her body grow warm with desire unless she was eager for his possession?

This woman could. He had to keep that in mind.

"Just checking," he said, his voice a lot cooler than his blood.

"Check again," she said quietly, "and so help me, I'll kill you."

"Keep something important from me again, and you won't be around long enough to try it." He picked up the pack and slung it over his shoulder. "My odds would be lots better if I didn't have you on my neck. Am I making myself clear?"

"Perfectly," Leanna said bitterly, and brushed past him.

It was a pathetic show of pride, but she should have known he wouldn't permit it. She'd only gone a couple of steps when he caught her arm.

"Those shoes."

She looked down at her feet. No sane woman would have chosen stiletto sandals for a hike in the desert but then, no sane woman would have chosen this man as her guide.

"What about them?"

"Take them off."

Her chin lifted. "Give me one good reason… Hey!"

A tug on her wrist and she was sitting on her rump. Cam knelt down and batted her hands away as he undid the straps of the sandals, snapped off the heels and handed the shoes back to her.

"Put them on and follow me. Every minute I have to stand around dealing with you is a minute wasted."

The "thank you" that had been hovering on her lips died.

Jaw set, she fell in behind him.

Cam's stride was long and he hadn't shortened it for his unwanted companion.

The sooner she got up to speed, the better.

She was a burden he hadn't asked for, but she was

his responsibility now. That was part of the code he'd lived by most of his adult life, but he couldn't think of any reason to tell her that. Let her worry about him abandoning her.

It might keep her from arguing so damned much.

To his surprise, she held to a steady pace for a long time. Well, why not? She was in good shape. Amazing shape.

Her body was her meal ticket.

Great shape or not, plodding through drifting sand was tough. Inevitably she began to fall behind. They couldn't afford to stop, but he couldn't afford to let her collapse, either. Not if they were going to reach what was rapidly starting to look like a real, honest-to-God hill before sunrise.

He came to a halt, slipped the pack off and fumbled inside it. He'd just found the water bottle when Salome plowed into him.

Cam caught her and held her steady. Her breathing was ragged and there was an unnatural flush in her cheeks.

And she was trembling. From exhaustion, from the night chill—either way, it was a bad sign. She could get her wind back if he sat her down, but the sand was cold. The only solution was to put his arms around her and draw her against him.

When she protested, he clucked his tongue in annoyance.

"Stop being an idiot," he growled. "Lean on me and catch your breath."

She didn't exactly melt into his embrace but after a few seconds, her shivering stopped.

"That's it. Let me warm you."

She nodded, and strands of her silky hair drifted over his lips. Cam tightened his arms around her.

He'd known all kinds of women in his life. He wasn't a fool: he knew that a beautiful woman could also be strong, but he hadn't expected it from Salome.

She looked delicate, but she'd held her own from the moment she'd threatened him with that ridiculous nail file. No tears. No complaints. No asking for favors because she was female.

Cam shut his eyes.

God, yes. She was very female. She even smelled good, a minor miracle because he doubted anyone could make such a claim for him. But Salome... Salome smelled of flowers. Vanilla. Woman.

The beat of her heart slowed as he stroked his hand up and down her back.

"I bet you could use a tall glass of orange juice."

Her sigh was almost a groan. "That's it. Torture me."

"And a steak." He kept one arm around her as he reached for the knapsack. "How do you like your steak, Salome? Rare? Well-done?"

"Rare," she said with a little sigh. "But charred on the outside."

"Why, ma'am," he said, putting on a drawl, "y'all must be from Texas, jest like me."

She looked up. "Are you really from Texas?"

"Uh-huh. Dallas."

"Aha. That's why you wear those boots."

"You mean, that's why I *wore* them," he said dryly. "But you're right. No self-respecting Texan goes anywhere without his boots."

She smiled. Cam wanted to applaud, which was ri-

diculous. Why did he give a damn if she smiled or not?
It just made sense to take her mind off their problems
for a little while.

"Here," he said. "Drink some water. More," he added,
when she began to give back the bottle. "Now for that
steak."

He held out the chunk of halvah. She took a delicate
bite. A tiny crumb adhered to her upper lip and she
swiped at it with the tip of her tongue, then closed her
eyes as the sweet taste bloomed on her tongue.

When she gave a little hum of pleasure, Cam remembered her making that same sound when he'd bared her
breasts and sucked her nipples into his mouth.

The candy was sweet, but the taste of her had been
sweeter.

His body sprang to full attention.

He swung away, tilted the water to his mouth for one
quick gulp, then capped the bottle and stuffed it into the
pack along with the remaining halvah.

"Okay," he said briskly, "time to move out."

"You didn't drink enough water. And you didn't eat
anything."

"I'm fine."

Leanna stared at Cam. He was telling the truth.
She'd been shaking with cold and exhaustion; her muscles were on fire and her feet, despite the clever thing
he'd done to her sandals, felt as if they were being
rubbed raw.

He had nothing on his feet. His T-shirt was insubstan-
tial. He'd set a killing pace but he didn't look as if this
was anything more than an easy stroll.

Maybe all those rippling muscles were for real.

"You—" She cleared her throat. "You do this kind of thing often?"

She sounded so serious that he didn't have the heart to laugh. "Well, let's see. Last time I escaped from a lunatic and crossed the desert with a beautiful woman was, oh, maybe two, three weeks ago. So I'd say, yeah, pretty often."

"I didn't mean…" She saw the laughter in his eyes. To heck with it, she thought, and laughed, too.

It was the first time he'd heard her laugh and it surprised him. A woman who'd come halfway around the world to play games with a sultan shouldn't have a laugh so delightfully earthy and innocent.

"I was talking about this. You know. Trudging across tough terrain without breathing hard. It seems second-nature to you."

He thought back to his years in Special Forces, then his years at the Agency. Nothing about those years had been second-nature. A man had to learn how to do all the things he'd done.

"I was a soldier for a long time."

"In this part of the world?"

"Among others." Cam frowned. She was shaking again. "You're still cold. Here." He reached out, grasped the lapels of the shirt and tugged her to him. "Button up. It'll help."

"I can do it," she said, but his fingers were already at the buttonholes, brushing lightly against her breasts. She inhaled sharply; he saw color race into her face, felt the answering rush of blood rush to his loins. Now, he thought. Right now. He could tumble her onto the sand, rip away the thong, bury himself inside her…

Salome took a step back.

"I'm fine," she said quickly. "All I need is to start moving again."

Silence fell between them. He felt a muscle jerk in his cheek. "Why?" he said hoarsely.

"Well, because of the energy I'll—"

"Why did you sell yourself to Asaad?"

She flinched, as if he'd struck her.

"It's an easy question. Why did you do it?"

Why did it hurt, to know he believed the worst about her?

"Were you desperate for money?"

"You mean, is my grandmother dying of some disease nobody's ever heard of? Is my mother about to lose the family homestead to a mustachioed villain?" Her eyes flashed. "Sorry. I'm fresh out of tearjerkers."

"For God's sake," he said roughly. "What kind of woman are you?"

"The kind who should have known better than to think you were different than your friend, the sultan."

She gasped as he pulled her to him. "You're right. I'm no different. A woman like you teases me with what she's got, I damned well intend to take it."

Cam's mouth captured hers. She tried to turn away but he was relentless, cupping her face, then sliding his hands down her back so he could lift her into him. She struggled hard and then, suddenly, she gave a wild little cry, wrapped her arms around his neck and opened her mouth to his.

Mercilessly, he plundered its sweetness, changing the angle of the kiss, taking it deeper and deeper while the last stars of the rapidly fading night wheeled over their heads.

He was the one who ended the kiss, clasping her wrists, easing her hands from his neck, bringing her palms to his mouth and biting lightly on the soft pads of flesh.

Then he took one of her hands and placed it over his throbbing erection.

"What happened in that bed isn't over, Salome. We both know it."

He took a last look at her. The softness of her mouth. The swift rise and fall of her breasts. Then he swung away, picked up the pack and began walking.

CHAPTER SIX

THEY reached the hill just as the sun rose.

"It's real," Leanna said softly. She spun toward Cam, eyes bright with excitement. "The mountain's real."

Cam grinned. "I wouldn't call it a mountain but yeah, it's as real as rain."

It damned well was. A little while ago, he'd started wondering if they were seeing the same mirage. Out here, anything was possible.

But the hill, the mountain, the heap of rocks and stunted trees, was directly ahead of them, and it was the closest thing yet to salvation.

"You up to a climb?"

Salome nodded. He could read exhaustion in her face but she was smiling. A pale gold curl hung over her temple and without thinking, he tucked it back behind her ear.

She was amazing, his Salome, and—

His Salome?

Cam's grin became a glower. He forced his eyes elsewhere. At the hill, at the sun, at the sand…

At her feet, where he found just the right distraction.

"For God's sake, your shoes are falling apart."

Her gaze followed his. Of course they were. Why did he sound so surprised?

"You can't climb those rocks like that."

Wordlessly she flashed a deliberate look at his bare feet.

"That's different," he snapped.

"How is it different?"

Cam's Special Forces training had involved walking barefoot over rougher terrain than this, but he didn't intend to explain himself to her.

"It's different because I say it is."

Her eyes narrowed. "Have you ever spent hours rehearsing a new dance routine?"

"What?"

"Dancing. Do you know anything about it?"

"No. Do you?"

His tone was hard and flat. So was the look on his face. A few minutes ago, she'd been thinking that only a man like Cameron Knight could have gotten them both this far.

How could she have been so stupid as to think nice things about him?

"Yes," she said coldly, "I do. If you knew anything at all about my profession—"

"Trust me, Salome. I know a lot about your profession."

Her hand whipped through the air. He caught it just before it connected with his jaw.

"Don't," he said softly. "Not unless you're prepared for the consequences."

"I wish I'd never laid eyes on you!"

"Right." His lips drew back from his teeth in a cold parody of a smile. "Except, according to you and Asaad, you'd be marching to your execution right about now."

"If you really believe that, you're a fool." Her voice trembled with tightly suppressed anger. "I'd be in the sultan's bed."

"I'm glad to hear you admit it."

"Why would I deny it? That's what Asaad wanted me for."

His mouth twisted. "The truth, at last."

"What would a man like you know about truth?"

Cam stared into her eyes for a long moment, torn between the desire to tell her that she was right, he didn't know a damned thing about truth—and the desire to pull her into his arms and kiss her. What was she doing to him, this witch? Salome wasn't a woman to whom you bared your soul.

"Enough talk," he growled. "You want to climb that rock pile? You need something more on your feet than what you have." He looked her over and his gaze settled on the thrust of her breasts. "Take off your bra."

She looked at him as if he'd lost his mind. "In your dreams."

Cam grabbed a fistful of her shirt and dragged her to her toes. "Take it off," he said softly, "or I will."

They stared at each other for a long minute. Then Leanna wrenched free.

"Your wish is my command," she said through her teeth.

Without taking her eyes from his, she did the trick learned by any girl who'd had to undress in a house shared with three brothers. Reach under your shirt, open your bra, tug at the straps, drag one down your arm and out the cuff of the shirt, then do the same with the other.

The look on Cam's face was priceless. "What the hell did you just do?"

"I took off my bra." She arched an eyebrow as she handed it to him. "Disappointed?"

Hell, no. Now he could see her nipples, perfectly outlined under the shirt, just waiting for the stroke of his hand.

The swift tightness in his groin infuriated him.

"Sit," he barked. She didn't move quickly enough to suit his temper. "Damn it, when I tell you something…"

He squatted, grabbed her ankle and tugged. Leanna landed on her backside.

"You're a hateful man."

"Lift your foot. Do it, or you can go up that mountain barefoot."

"I thought you said you wouldn't call it a mountain."

"It's whatever I say it is. Hold out those ribbons."

"What ribbons?"

Cam muttered something and grabbed a handful of the slender gold ribbons that hung from the thong. A bunch of small stones lay scattered at their feet. He chose one with a sharp edge and used it to slice the ribbons off. Then he tore the bra apart, wrapped her feet in the cups and tied them on with the ribbons.

"Oh," she said in a small voice.

He looked up. "Apology accepted."

"I didn't—" She swallowed. "You're right. I'm sorry."

He nodded, then stood up. "Okay. Let's do it. I want to be on the other side of that thing before the sun goes any higher."

The improvised shoes held, but the biggest surprise was what they found when they reached the top of the mountain.

Below them stretched a sea of grass and flowers…and beyond that, the gleaming white walls of an alabaster palace rose against a bright blue sky.

Amazing, how much faster it was going down than going up.

In no time, they were standing ankle-deep in the soft grass, listening to bird calls and feeling the gentle caress of a flower-scented breeze. It was like stepping from one plane of existence to another—but something about it made Leanna shudder.

"What's wrong?"

"Nothing." She blew out a breath. "Something. I'm just, I don't know. I'm—"

"Uneasy."

"Yes."

He reached for her hand. Without hesitation, she let him lace their fingers together.

"That's good," he said bluntly. "This is no time to let down our guard."

"I keep wondering whose palace that is…and if Asaad's men are there already, waiting for us."

"Yeah. Me, too."

"How do we find the answers?"

Cam swung toward her. "That's my job. You stay here while I—"

"No. And before you tell me to shut up and do as I'm told, just remember that I'm the one who got you into this mess."

"I'll let you in on a secret," he said, with a little smile. "I wasn't planning on testing Asaad's hospitality much longer."

"If I hadn't rushed things, you'd have had time to make a decent plan."

"Maybe." His hands came up and cupped her face. "But then I wouldn't have had as interesting a travel companion." He ran his thumb lightly over her mouth. "Trust me, baby. It's best if you stay here. I'll check things out and come back for you."

"No deal."

He thought about reminding her that they weren't making deals, but the stubborn set of her chin told him she'd made up her mind. Arguing would only waste time. Besides, for all he knew, she'd be safer with him.

"Okay. Come with me. Just stay close, and—"

"And?"

"And," he said huskily, "give me a kiss for luck."

She looked up into his eyes. They were a cool, brilliant green. What harm was there in just one kiss?

Cam let her press her mouth chastely to his. Then he caught her close and took her mouth so that he could taste her. Her arms went round his neck; when he parted her lips with his, she sighed and opened to him.

He held her for a long moment. When he finally let her go, her face was flushed and what he saw in her eyes made him want to kiss her again.

Instead he clasped her hand in his. "Ready?"

She nodded, and they began walking toward the alabaster palace.

"It's beautiful," Leanna whispered, "but I keep wondering who lives there. The Wizard…or the Wicked Witch?"

It was a good question. Cam could only hope the answer would be the one they needed.

The palace gates released at a touch. A flagstone path led to wide marble steps that ended at a pair of huge bronze doors.

"Cam?" Leanna whispered. "Where is everybody?"

The bronze doors swung slowly open.

"Get behind me," Cam said sharply, but the figure that appeared was far from threatening. It was a woman, slender and silver-haired, dressed in a flowing white robe. She made a deep curtsy, then rose, steepled her fingers and touched them to her forehead.

"Welcome, my lord."

Her voice was soft, her English clear and only lightly accented.

Cam squeezed Leanna's hand as he drew her forward. "What is this place?"

"You have arrived at the Palace of the Moon, my lord." The woman smiled at Leanna. "And my lady. Welcome to you, too. You have had a long journey."

"Thank you." Leanna's voice was strong but her hand trembled in Cam's. He put his arm around her and drew her close.

"I am called Shalla."

"Shalla," Cam said politely. "You seem to have been expecting us."

The woman gave a tinkling laugh. "Forgive me, sir. I should have realized you would have questions. Yes, we expected you. Our watchers in the turrets saw you approach. Besides, we are always prepared for the arrival of weary travelers. We are a sacred place, a haven between the dangerous lands of the western desert and the outer world."

It was a good story, maybe even a true one. Cam

knew that the myths and legends of antiquity were often grounded in reality.

"No one can come here to do evil, lord, unless that person is willing to bring down the vengeance of the gods."

"We're happy to hear it."

Shalla gestured to the open doors. "Please, come in. I will show you to your rooms. You can bathe and rest while your dinner is prepared."

Cam heard Salome sigh. It was the softest of sounds, but it held a world of longing. He couldn't ask her to keep going without food and rest. If nothing else, they could stay here long enough for her to recover from their forced march—and for him to try and contact the outside world.

He nodded, and they followed Shalla into the great entry hall of the Palace of the Moon.

Half a dozen steps inside, Salome stopped and stared in amazement. "Wow," she said softly.

She was right. *Wow* just about covered it. The only time Cam had been in a hall this large, he was twelve years old on a field trip to a museum.

The floor was black marble and shimmered with light pouring down from an open gold dome dozens of feet over their heads. Moorish arches stretched deep into the vast interior. A curved staircase climbed toward the second floor.

The palace was spectacular, a fantasy of color and texture, like something out of the Arabian Nights.

It was the kind of place a man brought a woman for days and nights of pleasure. He looked at Salome. Even now, her face smudged with dirt, her clothing in tatters, exhaustion burning like fire in her eyes, she was as beautiful as a dream.

How many other men had looked at her and thought the same thing?

And why in hell should it matter? He didn't give a damn who she'd been with or who she'd sold herself to. He hadn't sought out this place for some romantic fantasy. They'd stumbled across it out of sheer luck, and they'd make the most of their time here.

They needed rest. Food. Supplies. Most of all, he needed a plan that would get them back to civilization…

Cam's mouth thinned.

Who was he kidding? What he needed most was Salome, moving under him in bed. Her legs, wrapped around his hips. Her body, his for the tak—

"My lord? If you would follow me, please?"

Cam blinked. "Yes. Yes, of course."

This had to stop, he thought grimly, as they followed Shalla up the stairs. Salome was driving him crazy, and he didn't like it. Distraction was the last thing a man needed in this kind of situation.

There was only one way to solve the problem.

And the sooner it happened, the better.

CHAPTER SEVEN

SHALLA led them to a suite.

After two days in a filthy cell and a night trudging across the desert, Leanna would have seen paradise in anything with four clean walls and a window.

This looked like the top contender for Romantic Hideaway of the Year.

"Oh my," she breathed.

Cam took her hand as they strolled from room to room. "You took the words right out of my mouth, darling."

Darling? She looked at him as if he'd lost his mind. He smiled, brought her hand to his lips and kissed it. The look he flashed her was sharp. *Don't argue with me,* it said. *Just go along with whatever I say.*

The sitting room was elegant, bright with crystal vases and flowers. The bedroom's focal point was a massive bed draped in crimson and cream silk. Even the bathroom was spectacular, with frescoed walls, a white marble floor, golden swan fittings...and a sunken, black marble tub the size of a small lake.

"I hope this is to your liking, my lord."

Cam nodded, as if he'd expected to find such luxury in the tail end of nowhere.

"It's fine, thank you."

Leanna cleared her throat. "Actually…actually, I was wondering if there was a second bedroom somewhere in—"

Cam's fingers tightened on hers. "It's all right, love. I suspect Shalla has already figured out our secret."

She blinked at him. "Our—"

"I'm sure we're not the first lovers to elope and find shelter here. Isn't that right, Shalla?"

The silver-haired woman smiled. "You are correct, lord, and we are delighted by your presence. I will, of course, arrange for clothing and food to be brought to you."

"My lady and I are overwhelmed by your generosity. Isn't that right, darling?"

Only a fool would have disagreed. "Overwhelmed," Leanna replied.

Cam's smile disappeared as soon as he shut the door. "Alone at last," he said pleasantly, but his eyes were still filled with warning.

"Lovers? *Eloping* lovers? Are you cra—"

She gasped as he gathered her into his arms and kissed her. "Not another word," he whispered, his mouth against hers, "until I check things out."

"You mean, you think—" She bit her lip. "Oh."

"Yeah." His smile was glacial. "Oh."

She followed him from room to room, watched him examining the furniture, the lamps, even the moldings until he was satisfied.

"No bugs. No cameras. We're okay."

"You think Shalla lied about this being a sanctuary?"

"I think we'd be fools to take anything for granted."

"You're right. I should have thought of… What are you doing?"

"Getting undressed. I want a bath."

"Well, yes. So do I. But…"

"But," he said calmly, "you want to go first." He gave her a smile that didn't quite reach his eyes. "No problem, Salome. The tub's more than big enough for two."

"I am not taking a bath with…" Her breath caught. He was tugging his shirt free of his jeans. "Must you do that?"

"Do what?" He spoke calmly, but there was a tightness in his words.

"Get undressed as if I weren't here. It's—it's not polite."

"Give me a break, baby. I've had you beneath me with my hand between your legs. You really think I'm going to believe the sight of me taking my clothes off is too much for a lady like you?"

Her face blazed. "You're disgusting!"

She was right. He was going out of his way to offend her, and he was damned if he knew why…unless it was because he'd had it with her act, the way she pretended to be innocent when it suited her, then going wild in his arms when that seemed a better choice.

There was only one way to settle the tension between them, and he'd be damned if she was going to talk her way out of it.

"Come on," he said as he dumped his T-shirt on the floor. "Unbutton that shirt and…" His eyebrows drew together. She was staring at his left arm. "It's a tattoo. An eagle. Didn't you notice it before?"

Her eyes flew to his. "No."

"Take a closer look. It won't bite." A sexy smile angled across his mouth. "I might, but if I did, you'd like it."

He strolled toward her, deliberately flexing his arm so she could see the tattoo on his bicep in fuller detail. Naked to the waist, he was a magnificent sight.

Completely, gloriously male.

The eagle, wings spread, talons extended, golden eyes blazing, suited him to perfection.

"Well?" His voice was husky. "What do you think?"

Leanna tore her gaze from his and stared at the tattoo again. The eagle was a beautiful, deadly-efficient predator. Seeing it, she suddenly knew how its prey would feel as it swept down from the sky, the bone-deep realization that what came next was inevitable, that nothing in life could ever have as much meaning as being chosen by him, taken by him…

"Salome."

She jerked her head up. The look on Cam's face was as primitive as the pounding of her blood. He dropped the shirt, took a step forward, speared the fingers of one hand deep into her hair, tilted her head up and kissed her.

"No," she whispered, but she was already lifting herself to him, winding her arms around his neck, parting his lips so he could slip his tongue into her mouth.

"Like that," he said, bringing her closer, moving against her so she could feel how much he wanted her. "Just like that."

Her head fell back and he dipped his head and kissed the long line of her throat, nipped at the tender flesh, then soothed the tiny wound with a kiss.

Cam framed her face with his hands. Took tiny, biting kisses of her willing mouth. Swept his hands down her arms, then gathered her into a fierce embrace.

"Say it," he whispered. "Tell me, Salome. Tell me this is what you've waited for."

Leanna trembled. He was right. She wanted him. Wanted this. Had wanted it from his first caress. He was her knight, and she was—

She was his Salome.

That was the woman he wanted. A seductress who lived for the pleasure of the flesh, who could play the game with him and never look back.

Was that the kind of man she wanted to take her virginity?

"No. Cam." She twisted against him, but he didn't stop. His hands were under her shirt, cupping her backside, lifting her, lifting her... "Stop it," she said, her voice sharp with panic. "I don't want to do this!"

At first, she thought he hadn't heard her, or didn't want to hear her. Then, after what seemed a long, long time, his arms dropped to his sides.

"You play dangerous games, Salome."

His eyes were as cold and hard as green glass. For the first time since he'd tossed her out of the Hummer, Leanna felt a curl of fear in her belly, but she knew better than to show it.

If you weren't strong enough to fight off an eagle's attack, you needed the courage to face it.

"I made a mistake."

"Damned right, you did."

"I realized that—that I didn't want to do this. I want—"

She cried out as he grasped her wrist and jerked her arm behind her back.

"I know exactly what you want," he growled. "Me, crawling up the wall because you've teased me so long my brain's turned to mush."

"You're wrong! And you're hurting me." Desperately, she tried to wrench free. "Let me go! If you don't—"

"What? You'll scream?" He laughed. "No matter what Shalla hears coming from this room, she won't do a thing. Nothing's changed in this part of the world in a thousand years, Salome. Mention women's rights around here, you'll draw a blank look." His smile faded; he lowered his head until their faces were inches apart. "I'm in charge. You're disposable. Got that?"

Salome's face had lost all its color. She was trying her best to stand up to him but she was shaking like a leaf.

Hell, he thought, and let go of her with an exaggerated lifting of his hands, as if he'd just realized he was touching something he'd never intended to touch.

"I'm finished with this crap, Salome. Take your bath, do whatever the hell you want. Just be sure you keep away from me because if you try playing games again, I promise you, I'll win."

A sob burst from her throat as she flew past him.

He almost laughed.

Anybody watching this little scene would have thought she was a virgin running for her life. And that he, without question, was the villain.

The bathroom door slammed. The bolt shot home, loud as the crack of a rifle. Who gave a damn? It was a meaningless gesture anyway. Did she really think a lock would protect her if he changed his mind?

Cam folded his arms and glared at the door.

How come he couldn't hear the water running in the tub? Because, he thought grimly, because she was probably leaning against the wall, laughing now that he'd tumbled for her latest routine.

She'd been turning him on and off like a machine since he'd first set eyes on her.

A muscle knotted in his jaw.

And he'd been idiot enough to let her do it.

He swung away from the locked door, paced the bedroom like a tiger trapped in a cage. Too bad he hadn't been keeping score. By now, it was probably zero for the home team and one hundred for hers.

Still no sound of running water. She was in there, laughing at her latest victory and he was out here, leaving footprints in the carpet.

But it would get old, after a while. She'd tire of enjoying herself at his expense. She'd turn on the water and take off her tattered clothes. The shirt. Then the thong. She'd pin up that silken mass of hair that tumbled in golden waves over her breasts.

Suddenly the room seemed airless.

If he believed the sultan, he'd saved her pretty neck from the chopping block. He'd gotten her out of Baslaam. And how did she show her thanks?

He glared at the locked door.

By teasing him until he was as desperate as a teenage boy with one hand on a Playmate centerfold and the other on his—

Cam roared with rage and slammed his shoulder into the door. Once. Twice.

The wood gave way and he burst into the room.

Leanna came at him like a wildcat. He feinted. Ducked. Grunted as she caught him in the gut with an elbow. She was quick and strong and maybe she could have fought another man off…

But not him.

He was crazed with anger, with frustration, with needing what he had been too long denied. In some dark recess of his mind, he knew he'd crossed that thin line between civilization and the jungle but he didn't care.

Nothing would stop him from finishing what she had started.

"I'll kill you!" she panted. "So help me God, you do this and I'll—"

He caught her wrists in one hand, pinned them above her head and used his body to jam her against the wall. He plunged a hand into her hair, wound a thick length of it around his fist and took her mouth with his, kissing her mercilessly, nipping her tender flesh, thrusting his tongue between her lips when she gasped for breath.

She fought hard, sank her teeth into his bottom lip and drew blood, but it didn't matter. Tonight, at last, he was going to get what she'd promised.

"Bastard," she hissed. "No good, rotten ba—"

She cried out as he pushed his knee between her thighs, lifting her off the floor so that the long, thick ridge of his erection pressed against the female heart of her.

"Remember what I asked you that first time? I'm asking it again. How do you want this? I can make it good for you, or I can take you hard and fast, zip up and walk away."

A shudder raced the length of her body. "Oh, God! Cameron—Cameron…"

There was something in the way she said his name. Something he'd never heard before in a woman's voice. Something that said her fear masked a different emotion, one she wasn't ready to confront.

Even in his out of control fury, he heard it.

"Salome," he whispered…and she shuddered and raised her face blindly to his.

"Cam," she said again, and he groaned, gathered her close and kissed her. Kissed her with a mix of hunger and tenderness. He said her name again. Then he swept her into his arms and carried her to the bed.

He lay her back against the pillows. Her eyes shone with tears, but now they glittered like stars. Her mouth was pink and swollen from his kisses.

Cam's heart turned over.

He'd lied to her. To himself. He'd never have taken her through force. He wanted this. Needed this. Her, asking for his possession. Burning for him as he burned for her.

"Tell me," he said, just as he had before… Except, this time he knew what her answer would be.

"Cameron." Her lips curved in a tremulous smile as she raised her arms to him. "Please. Make love to me."

He came down on the bed beside her and reached for the buttons on her shirt. He opened one. Then another, but his fingers felt clumsy and he growled in frustration, grasped the edges of the cotton fabric and tore it open, baring her breasts.

He'd seen them before. Touched them. Then, he'd pretended it didn't matter. Now, he wanted her to know that nothing mattered more.

"You're beautiful," he said as he bent to her, kissed

her pale gold flesh, licked an apricot nipple and then drew it into his mouth.

She gave a little cry and arched toward him.

"So beautiful," he said, and slid his hand under the golden thong.

She was hot. Wet. For him, only for him. She moaned his name as he found the swollen bud within her honeyed folds and stroked it.

Her eyes went dark with pleasure, and he damned near lost control.

Slow down, his head whispered, but his body was on a timetable of its own. He couldn't wait. Not anymore.

He'd take her quickly this first time. Just unzip his jeans, enter her. Drive her up and up, fly with her into the sun. Then he'd make slow love to her, discover all the things that excited her, watch her face as she came, then let go and empty himself inside her…

Oh, God! His head snapped back as the awful truth hit home.

He had no condoms.

"Cam? Cam, what's the matter?"

He looked down into her eyes, pools of deepest blue in the soft light of late afternoon, and let himself think what it would be like to enter her without protection. Slide deep into all that heat. Ride her, bareback.

Just the thought drove him dangerously close to the edge. Carefully, ignoring her whimper of protest, he sat back.

"We can't do this," he said gruffly.

"But I thought—I thought we both wanted—"

He leaned forward and kissed her, hard.

"We do, sweetheart. But I don't have a condom."

"A con…" Her face turned red. "Oh."

"Yeah." For a second, he wished he were seventeen again, a kid with a constant hard-on and a rubber always tucked in his wallet.

"But you don't…" She hesitated. He could see her throat constrict as she swallowed, almost as if the intimacy of their talk embarrassed her. "You don't need one. It's—it's safe."

Safe? No way. Calendar roulette wasn't his speed.

"I'm on the pill, Cam. Because—because my cycle's irregular. That happens to some dancers."

He felt his belly knot. Why go through such a convoluted explanation when they both knew damned well why she was on the pill?

"It's from all the exercise."

Oh, yes. She probably got a lot of exercise.

"It's not one of those pills you have to take every day, so—"

"And a good thing it's not," he said coldly, welcoming his anger, knowing it was far safer than whatever he'd come close to feeling a couple of minutes ago. Smiling tightly, he rolled away from her. "Thanks. But there's more to consider than calendars."

"You mean—you mean, the possibility of—of disease?"

He wanted to shake her until her teeth rattled. She sounded as innocent as a schoolgirl. How in hell could he have forgotten what a fine actress she was?

"Yes," he said coldly. "That's exactly what I mean."

"I don't—I mean, I can't—I mean…" Her color deepened. "Cam? I'm not—"

"Yeah. I'm sure you're not. You probably have a health

department certificate to prove it." He bared his teeth. "Where are those things when a girl needs them, hmm?"

Her face went from pink to white in a heartbeat. "You son of a bitch!"

"Lay off the name-calling for a while, okay? I'm tired of it. Just go take your bath. I'll see about that meal Shalla promised us."

"I'd sooner starve than eat with—"

But Leanna was talking to herself.

Cam had already stormed from the room.

Go take your bath? Was that really what he'd said?

Cameron Knight couldn't speak a sentence without turning it into an order.

Besides, she'd sooner have stayed sweaty and dirty than climb into that obscene tub. The basin, hot water, soap and a washcloth would do just fine.

Clean, skin almost raw from all the scrubbing—as if it were possible to scrub away the unseen imprint of a man's hands—Leanna opened a closet in the bathroom and found it filled with silky gowns—caftans, she supposed—in a rainbow of colors. She chose one blindly and slipped it over her bare skin, buttoning it from her throat to her toes. There were matching slippers, too, but when she tried putting her feet into them, she winced. The toes on her left foot were tender.

Better to go barefoot than risk an injury that might affect her dancing, she thought...and almost laughed. Dancing again was the least of her worries. First, she'd have to get out of this place alive. It killed her to admit, but she knew she'd never be able to do it alone.

If Cam had abandoned her...

No. She wasn't going to jump to conclusions. Wasn't there some old saying about not borrowing trouble ahead of time?

A small lacquered box held ivory hairpins. Leanna pulled her hair into a loose topknot and pinned it in place.

The bathroom door was still on its hinges, though it hung drunkenly in its frame. She opened it cautiously. The bedroom was empty. So was the sitting room. Someone had been here, though. The room was bright with candlelight; a long table held an assortment of food and drink.

Leanna filled a crystal goblet with water and sipped at it as she stepped through a pair of French doors onto a wide stone balcony.

The moon hung like a cameo against a black velvet sky that blazed with the fire of a billion stars. Gardens stretched in every direction, their flowers delicately scenting the night. Below the terrace, torches illuminated a curving azure pool.

The setting was blissful but even the set for a ballet was more real than this. Cameron Knight wasn't a prince any more than she was a princess, waiting to be awakened by his kiss. The things that had made him seem so attractive here, where survival depended on his testosterone levels, would be a turnoff anywhere else.

She was embarrassed even thinking it, because she wasn't proud of it, but the truth was, sleeping with him would have been—it would have been the equivalent of going slumming.

Cam had none of the qualities she'd ever wanted in a man. He'd dented her pride but she'd—but she'd—

Leanna caught her breath. She stepped back into the shadows. Cam was heading toward the pool, strolling along as if he owned the world.

What was he doing?

Unhurriedly he stripped off his T-shirt. Didn't it occur to him that someone might be watching? That she—

Her mouth went dry as he stepped out of his jeans.

God, he was beautiful! The hard, dangerous face. The black hair, long and curling lightly at his nape. The wide shoulders and broad chest, taut abdomen…

Her eyes danced lower.

He was still aroused. Incredibly aroused.

Desire flooded her senses. There was no point in lying to herself. She'd never admit it to him—she'd never have to—but how could a woman see this man and not want him?

He stepped to the edge of the pool, then dived in. The water hardly rippled. A second passed. Then his head broke the surface. He swam the pool's length, jackknifed and swam it again, over and over until she lost count.

At last, he hoisted himself out of the water. As he did, he looked up at the terrace. Leanna's heart stopped. Then she remembered that he couldn't see her.

But she could see him.

All that exercise hadn't done a thing to lessen his frustration.

Wouldn't it be lovely if she could find a way to make it worse? He'd accused her of deliberately teasing him, but she hadn't.

She hadn't.

Because if she had, if she really wanted to drive him crazy…

Don't do it, Leanna. She heard the little whisper inside her, loud and clear. *Leanna, don't!*

She watched as he put on his jeans. Folded his arms. Stared up at the balcony, even though he couldn't see her.

Leanna took a deep breath. Closed her eyes. Let the music start to play in her mind. It was the "Bolero." She loved listening to it but she had never danced to it.

Not surprising, considering that she danced ballet.

What she danced on this night would not be ballet. It would be a dance of her own creation, designed to show a man she despised exactly what he'd missed.

Slowly she stepped from the shadows into the moonlight. The night turned still, as if the world were holding its breath. She looked down, watched Cam's expression change when he saw her.

Something hot and wild skittered through her blood.

Eyes shut, head lifted, she swayed and dipped to music only she could hear. Her head fell back. Her body arched. She raised her arms to the moon as the beat of the music and the beat of her heart became one.

The tempo quickened. She brought her hands to the first button of the caftan. Slowly, still swaying, she undid the buttons until the garment hung open on her shoulders, exposing her naked body to the night...

To the man who watched her.

The primordial pulse of the music filled her senses. Leanna took the pins from her hair and let it tumble over her shoulders in golden waves. She raised her hands to her breasts and cupped them, then let her palms drift down the curves of her body, over her belly, to her thighs.

The music reached fever pitch. She stood absolutely

still. Slowly, as the last note faded into the night, she let the caftan slide to the floor, the fabric sighing against her sensitized flesh like a lover's whisper.

Naked, she lifted her arms to the moon—and knew she had not danced to torment the man watching her.

She had danced to seduce him.

Silence hung on the night breeze. Then she heard Cam speak her name.

"Salome."

She opened her eyes and looked down. Too late. He was already moving, disappearing as he rounded the pool.

He was coming for her.

The sitting room door flew open. She spun toward the sound and saw him as he came into the room. She could almost feel the heat coming off him, smell the scent of his maleness.

All at once, she was afraid. Her hands flew to her breasts and groin in an age-old gesture of protection.

"Wait," she whispered. "Cam—"

He slammed the door and started toward her, kicking aside a chair that stood in his way. When he reached her, he caught her in his arms.

"No more waiting, Salome," he said roughly, and took her down to the silk carpet.

"Cam," she said, "Cam—"

But he was beyond hearing her. Beyond rational thought. He kissed her, shoved his knee between her thighs, caught her wrists and pinned her arms high over her head.

"Watch me," he said. "I want to see your face as I take you."

He entered her on one long, hard thrust. Leanna

cried out and his body shuddered, then went completely still.

God, he thought, *God, could it be true?*

His Salome was a virgin.

CHAPTER EIGHT

A VIRGIN?

The woman who'd come to him dressed like a *houri?* Who had come to Baslaam as Asaad's sexual toy?

There was no mistaking the fragile barrier that shielded her from Cam's full penetration.

Sweat beaded his forehead. Every muscle in his body screamed with tension as he fought against sinking into her.

"Salome," he said hoarsely, "why didn't you tell me?"

"I tried. Before. When you said you didn't have a condom, but—"

"Ah, God, what a fool I've been."

"Shh. It doesn't matter. Just—just—" She moved. A delicate shift of her hips, but it was enough to make him close his eyes and groan.

"Don't—don't do that, sweetheart. Just—just hold still. I'll pull back and you—" The breath hissed between his teeth. She'd shifted again, lifting toward him with such subtlety he might have imagined it.

But he hadn't.

She wanted him.

The realization filled him with a joy so fierce it

shocked him. His golden dancer had never lain in a man's arms. Now, she lay in his.

And she wanted him.

But she was a virgin. A virgin. As rare a gift as a man could find in this upside-down, often brutal world.

How could he take her innocence? She wasn't thinking straight. The danger. The adrenaline rush. No, she wasn't thinking straight and besides…

Besides, he didn't deserve her gift.

She was brave and strong and beautiful, his Salome, and her virginity belonged to someone else, not someone like him. Not a man who knew more of the world's evil than he could ever forget.

If had did one right thing in his life, it would be this.

"Cam?"

Her whisper was filled with questions, but he had the only answer that made sense. Slowly, slowly, he began to withdraw from her.

"No," she said, and her muscles tightened around him.

His heart thundered in his chest. Could a man die of pleasure? Of doing the right thing?

"Shh," he murmured. "It's all right, sweetheart."

A shudder racked his body as he made the final separation from her. She whimpered in protest and he brushed his mouth lightly over hers.

"Salome," he said softly. "Forgive me."

"You couldn't have known."

"I should have listened to you, sweetheart, but I was too damned stubborn."

"Then, listen to me now." Her eyes met his. "I don't want you to stop." She framed his face with her hands. "I want you to make love to me, Cam. I want you inside me."

Her plea was a torment. Somehow, he managed to shake his head.

"You think this is what you want, but it isn't."

"Damn you, Cameron." The words were harsh, but her voice shook and tears glittered in her eyes. "Don't you want me?"

Cam wrapped the caftan around her and drew her into his arms. Holding her close, he rocked her against him.

"More than I've ever wanted anything in my life."

"Then why—"

"Because I'm everything you said I was. Every name you called me." He lifted her face, stroked her hair back from her temples. "You deserve someone better."

"No! Don't say that. You—"

"Just let me hold you, baby. Come on. Lean against me."

The seconds crept by. He could feel her body softening against his. Finally she sighed.

"I understand. Girls talk. Some of them say—they say virginity is a burden."

"The hell it is!" He clasped her shoulders and held her just far enough from him so he could look into her eyes. "It's a gift, Salome. That's why—" His voice roughened. "That's why I just want to hold you in my arms. Why I wish to God I could take back all the things I accused you of."

"You believed Asaad. I don't blame you. He made it all sound logical."

"I should have seen the truth right away. You risked your life, warning me that he was setting me up." He paused. "How did it happen?" He felt a tremor go through her and silently cursed himself for asking her to relive what were surely ugly memories. "Never mind, baby. I shouldn't have asked."

"It's all right. I want to tell you. Maybe saying it all out loud will make it seem less real." Leanna swallowed dryly. "I was with a dance troupe on a tour through eastern Europe. One day, during rehearsal, a couple of the other girls and I stepped outside the theater for some air. A van pulled up. Some men jumped out. They grabbed us and—and stuffed us into the back. I thought they were going to kill us but one girl said—she said they were slavers and—and—"

"And," Cam said grimly, "she was right."

Leanna nodded. "Asaad bought me. He was going to—he was going to use me but then you showed up. He told me he'd set me free if I—if I did things with you. I knew he was lying but you were an American. And I figured—"

"You figured I was riding in on a white horse to save you," he said gruffly, "except it turned out I was just an American version of Asaad."

"No!" She pulled back in his arms and shook her head. "You're nothing like him, Cameron. You saved my life. If you hadn't come to Baslaam, if you hadn't escaped and taken me with you…"

He smiled. "I think you've got that backward, sweetheart. *You* escaped. I just went along for the ride."

She smiled, as he'd hoped, and some of the darkness left her eyes.

She was one amazing woman, his dancer.

If only they'd met half a world away. At a party. If

only they'd met in a way that hadn't vividly reminded him of why he didn't deserve a woman like her.

Maybe it was just as well.

Another time, another place, he'd have said to hell with gallantry or whatever it was coursing through him right now. Salome was beautiful and bright, qualities he couldn't have resisted. He'd have gone into full pursuit. Sent her flowers, taken her to dinner, kissed her at her door, whispered that he hated to leave her and she'd have invited him in.

They'd have gone to bed, he'd have said all the right things except the thing he knew better than to believe in. The thing she deserved.

After a few weeks or maybe a couple of months, he'd have walked away. It was all very civilized and the women who moved in and out of his life knew the rules.

Salome didn't, and he'd be damned if he'd be the man who introduced her to the game.

He just wished she didn't feel so wonderful in his arms.

Carefully he shifted his weight. Chivalry could only take you so far. If he hadn't moved, the evidence of his still-rampant desire would be all too obvious.

Gently he lifted her face to his and kissed her.

"You know what?" he said, smiling.

"What?"

"If I don't eat something soon, my ribs are gonna say hello to my backbone."

She laughed. "How come I keep forgetting you're a Texas boy at heart?"

"No joke, sweetheart. I'm starved. How about you?"

Her stomach growled in response. Cam chuckled and turned his back as he slipped into his jeans and rose to his feet. "Come on, little lady. Let's see if we can find ourselves some good ol' barbecue in that spread Shalla provided."

His Salome laughed as he drew her to her feet. Smiling, he kept his eyes on her face as he buttoned her caftan but when his knuckles accidentally brushed her skin, he bit back a groan.

Sweet Jesus, how was he going to survive this night?

They sat at a round glass table on the balcony, talking as they ate. Then, gradually, Salome fell silent. Cam put down his plate and reached for her hand.

"Hey," he said softly. "Why so sad?"

Because none of this would last. Because he really was the beautiful prince who'd stumbled across a sleeping princess. Because she knew, as well as he did, that they might not survive.

Because if she were going to leave this earth, she wanted to know she had, if only for a little while, belonged to Cameron Knight.

"Sweetheart?"

Leanna reached out and touched her fingers to his face. He caught her hand and pressed his lips to her palm.

"Cam." She took a long breath. "I want to ask you something. If you don't want to do it…if you think I'm being too forward…"

"Salome. Ask me anything you want."

"You said—you said you don't want to sleep with me."

"No." He cleared his throat. "What I said was, I can't sleep with you, baby. God knows I want to."

"But there are—I mean, there are other things…"

Her face turned pink as her voice trailed away. He

stared at her and thought of those other things, and knew he'd never be strong enough to live through them.

"Salome. Sweetheart, you're right, there are other things. But I'm not a saint. If I put my mouth on…" Holy hell. Just the image was going to make him come. "If I do those other things, I'm afraid I'll—that I'll—"

"We could take a bath together."

The words came out so swiftly that at first, he wasn't sure he understood what she'd said. He ran them over in his mind, sorted them out…

"A bath?" For the first time since he'd turned thirteen, Cam's voice broke. "Together?"

"Yes. In that big old tub. You in one end. Me in the other. Lots of bubbles so nobody can see anything and—and—" Leanna buried her face in her hands. "Oh God, don't look at me that way! I'm sorry. I never should have—"

Cam caught her hands and drew them down. "It's a great idea," he said bravely.

"It is?"

"Yes." He swallowed. "You take the bath. I'll keep you company."

Her smile dimmed. "That's not the same thing."

Damned right, it's not, he thought, but he only smiled.

There was a chaise longue in the bathroom.

Cam settled into it as Salome ran her bath. He'd turn his back when the time came. For now, surely there was no harm in watching her turn on the taps, or choose a bath oil from tiny crystal vials that lined a shelf near the tub.

Nobody could fault him, either, for watching her lift her hair from her shoulders and secure it with a pin so that soft tendrils drooped against her neck.

"Perfect," she said.

Perfect, he thought, and winced at the swift clench-ing of his body.

Her back was to him. He could tell she was undoing the buttons on the caftan. It slid from her shoulders.

It was time to look away.

But he didn't. His eyes were riveted to the graceful lines of her back.

"Cam?" she said softly. "The tub's so deep... Could you help me get in?"

He nodded. It was safer than speaking, he thought as he went to her. If he kept his eyes averted, if she didn't turn around...

But she did.

Slowly, slowly enough to make his heart stop, she turned and faced him.

"Cam?" she whispered.

All the questions a woman could ask a man swam in her eyes. All the answers he wanted to give her pounded through his blood.

Slowly he let his gaze slide to her breasts. Her belly. To the nest of golden curls at the juncture of her thighs.

He remembered the feel of those curls against his hand. What would they feel like against his mouth? He wanted to press his face against her, draw her scent deep into his lungs. Open her to him, watch her face as he kissed her...

"Salome," he said softly, "you're trying to seduce me."

"I tried that once," she said, just as softly. "And it didn't work."

And now, they both knew, she was trying again. He didn't know whether to laugh or cry. She had never been with a man; he had been with who knew how many women, and she thought she could seduce him?

He was tougher than that—and tough men weren't cowards. He thought of what she'd asked him before, if there weren't other things they could do instead of what they both wanted.

There were. Things that would give them both some moments of sweet pleasure without killing him, and perhaps even offer her some release.

Cam smiled. He undid his jeans and stepped out of them. Then he lifted his dancer in his arms and stepped down into the water.

All he had to do now was lower her to her feet. Make sure he set the pace…

Somehow, her arms wound around his neck.

Somehow, when he sank into the tub, she ended up on his lap.

He had to move her. Just a little. If she stayed where she was—oh, God, right where she was…

He shifted her. Bad idea. Her bottom was so warm against him. So female…

Another little shift. Better. Not great, but an improvement.

"Right," he said, "how's that feel?"

Salome sighed. "Wonderful."

Were they talking about the water? Or were they talking about his straining flesh, swollen and aching against her?

"The water's so soothing."

Good. They were talking about the water. She was, anyway.

"It's magic," she whispered.

She was the magic. She felt so soft in his arms. So right. Her head was against his shoulder and her eyes were closed, her lashes dark crescents against her cheeks. The ends of her hair were wet and trailed over her breasts like drifts of gold and her mouth...

Her mouth looked like a flower petal.

Cam bent his head, brushed his mouth lightly over hers. "Sweet," he whispered.

She tilted her chin up. Her lips parted. Her mouth clung to his and he felt his blood thunder in his ears.

"I'm going to bathe you now, Salome."

His voice was rough as gravel. His heart was racing. Gently he lifted her from his lap and stood her between his legs. Then he reached for one of the washcloths stacked on the tub's ledge.

He dipped it in the water.

"First your face," he whispered. "And your throat." She closed her eyes. "And then—and then—" Slowly he ran the cloth over her breasts. He felt her tremble. He was trembling, too, as he took the cloth lower, over her belly, lower, lower...

The cloth fell from his fingers. He bent his head, kissed her breasts as he slipped his hand between her thighs. She whimpered and his touch lingered, centered on that one forbidden place.

"That feels..." Her head fell back. "That feels..."

"Does it?" His voice was raw. His body was on fire. "How does it feel, Salome?"

She sighed. He increased the friction. Warned himself that this was only for her. For her. Not for him. Not for—

Her cry rose into the night. Pleasure, fierce and elemental, rushed through him. He had done this. Given her this.

A feeling so deep, so intense it terrified him shot through his heart.

Quickly he got to his feet. Lifted his golden dancer in his arms. Stepped from the tub with her clinging to his neck, with his mouth drinking from hers. Gently he set her on her feet. Wrapped her in an enormous towel.

Then he kissed her again, lifted her again. Carried her from the bathroom to the bed, where he laid her down as carefully as if she were the most precious treasure in the universe.

"Don't leave me," she whispered.

Never, he thought fiercely. He would never leave her again.

"Shh," he said, and kissed her.

He locked the sitting room door, then jammed a chair under it. The bedroom door had no lock; a chair alone would have to do.

By the time he came back to the bed, Salome was asleep.

He sat down next to her, smiling as he watched her. She lay on her back, her hair spread over the silk pillows.

She was the portrait of goodness and innocence.

And somewhere out in the vast wilderness that surrounded this place, Asaad was searching for her.

Cam's smile faded.

Gently so he wouldn't waken her, he kissed her mouth. Then he lay down beside her, drew the comforter over them both and gathered her into his arms.

Salome sighed and lay her head on his shoulder. Cam lifted her hand and kissed it.

Then he closed his eyes and fell asleep.

CHAPTER NINE

LEANNA awoke alone in the big bed. The inky darkness of the room was filled with a silence so complete she could hear the sound of her own heartbeat.

"Cam?"

No answer.

"Cam?" she said again.

Her eyes began adjusting to the darkness. The door to the sitting room was open. Through it, she could see Cam standing out on the balcony.

She let out a relieved breath, started to push aside the comforter—and stopped.

Maybe he needed time alone.

She didn't. She needed only to be with him, but there was no reason for him to feel the same way, especially after what had happened in the tub.

Her face burned.

Maybe he was disgusted with her.

She couldn't believe she'd been so bold. Sex had never much interested her. Dance was a harsh taskmaster. It left you with little time or energy for anything else, but then she'd met Cameron Knight...

And she'd fallen in love with him.

114

Her heart did a little flip-flop.

How could that be? She'd only known him a handful of hours. Yes, but they'd lived a lifetime in those hours.

Who knew how much time they had left?

Leanna sat up and threw the comforter aside. She wasn't going to worry about what Cam thought of her. Time was too precious to waste.

There was a robe at the foot of the bed. She put it on, tied the sash and made her way across the bedroom, through the sitting room, toward Cam. She stopped when she was almost at the French doors and let her eyes drink him in.

He stood with his feet apart, his hands clamped around the terrace railing. He'd put on his jeans though he hadn't zipped them up. She could tell by the way they hung low on his hips.

Her gaze moved over his muscled shoulders and down the long lines of his naked back.

My beautiful warrior, she thought, and smiled.

"Cameron?" she said softly.

"Salome," he said, and she could tell, from the one word, that he'd known she was there. Of course. He was too good at what he did not to have heard her.

She wanted to run into his arms, but he'd turned to face her and there was something in the rigidity of his posture that made her hold back.

"Did I wake you?" he asked.

"No. No, I—I—"

"Come here," he said roughly. He held out his arms and everything changed, the way he was looking at her, the way he held himself, the heaviness that had suddenly settled in her heart.

She flew to him and he gathered her against him. The night was cool but his skin was warm. The scent of the oil she'd used in the bath clung to him, mixing with the aroma she loved best, the one that was all his own.

Leanna burrowed closer. Cam closed his eyes. God, she felt wonderful in his arms.

"Um." She sighed and kissed his shoulder. "Aren't you cold, standing out here?"

"I'm fine." His voice grew husky. "Here. Let me warm you."

Cam undid the sash of her robe and slid his hands beneath it. Her skin was silken; she stretched against him and made a sound like a purring cat.

"Nice," she whispered.

Nice, indeed. He really had intended only to warm her but, damn it, his traitorous body was going to make a liar of him again. He shifted his weight, turned a little away from her in hopes she wouldn't discover the truth.

She tilted her face to his. "Have you been awake long?"

He shrugged. "Just a little while."

"What woke you?"

Questions, he thought, questions that had no answers. Where was Asaad? Had he found their trail yet? And then there was the most important question of all.

How would he save his Salome?

She didn't need to hear any of that. They'd found a peaceful oasis and there was no need to give it up just yet.

"I was thirsty," he said. "I got up for a drink of water. What woke you?"

Color rose in her cheeks but her eyes stayed on his. "I missed you."

He drew her to him and kissed her. Then he enfolded

her in his arms again and rested his chin on the top of her head. Maybe he was wrong. This might be the time to tell her a little of what was on his mind.

"I figured, as long as I was awake, I'd go out and take a look around."

"Outside? You should have taken me with you. Suppose something had happened?"

"Nothing did," he said, loving the courage of her response. "We're safe enough here."

"For a while."

Part of him wanted to lie, but lies wouldn't protect her.

"Yes," he said. "For a while. I wanted to look around while the rest of the place slept. I figured, the fewer eyes watching, the better."

"And? What did you find?"

He hesitated. His dancer deserved the truth.

"This place is like that mystical kingdom. Shangri-La. I don't think it's been touched by the world in at least a hundred years."

She leaned back in his arms. "Why do I get the feeling that isn't good?"

"Because there's nothing here we can use," he said bluntly. "No cars, no trucks, no telephone. Not even a radio."

"You have a cell phone. And we found that GPS."

He'd already tried the freaking cell phone in the desert, on the mountain, outside the palace a little while ago, right after he'd taken a reading with the GPS. One lonely transmission bar had appeared on the cell's screen. He'd punched the speed dial button for his office, rattled off the coordinates from the GPS to the office voice mail, but the solitary bar had vanished before he'd finished.

Yes, but his Salome's eyes were full of hope. Was a lie by omission really a lie?

"Sure. We can try them in the morning."

"Good," she said, and smiled at him.

Cam was lying. Leanna could hear the deceit in his too-cheerful tone, but she'd go along with it. He was lying to protect her. That was the kind of man he was.

He was the man she'd waited for, saved herself for, though she hadn't known it.

It wasn't as if she'd made a conscious effort to keep her virginity. It was just that between school and ballet, there hadn't been much time for boys. Now there was even less. Rehearsals and performances took all her energy and time.

Plus, the men she'd met throughout her career were complete turnoffs.

In Vegas, where she'd danced to earn enough quick money to finance a move to New York, the men had mostly been sharpies, accustomed to buying whatever they wanted.

In Manhattan, she met men in love with their own images.

The city was what had won her heart. It was where classical ballet lived and breathed, where she'd failed an audition for the New York Ballet but won a coveted spot with Ballet Manhattan.

She was too busy for men anyway. Still, there'd been times she'd wondered if she were normal. If her hormones were okay because sex just didn't seem a priority item.

Then she'd fallen into a nightmare, been rescued by a tough-talking stranger and discovered she not only wanted him to teach her about sex, but she wanted him to look into her eyes and say that he loved her.

Such foolishness.

She was too old to believe in miracles.

Cam didn't love her. He wouldn't love her…but that didn't mean she couldn't love him. Now. Tomorrow. Forever.

"Hey."

She blinked and looked up at him.

"Such a long face, sweetheart." He put his finger under her chin and tilted her face to his. "There's nothing to worry about. Come morning, we'll check things out." He forced a smile. "You know that old saying. It's always darkest before the dawn."

"You don't have to protect me from the truth, Cam. I know we're in a tough spot."

"We are, but I'll come up with something."

"You already did. You saved my life."

"I told you, you're the one who did the lifesaving. If you hadn't let out that blood-curdling shriek, I'd still be standing in that bathroom."

"No, you wouldn't," she said, smiling. "What I said before is the truth. You'd have escaped, but with a plan."

"What I said is the truth, too. I wouldn't have had you with me."

"Meaning, your chances would be lots better."

"Wrong. One hundred percent wrong. How'd you come up with that?"

"You'd have made better time alone."

"Not true. You kept to a pace would have made most guys drop."

A smile tilted across her lips. "You mean it?"

"Damned right, I mean it." He bent his head and brushed a kiss on her lips. "I should know, Salome. I do this for a living."

"This?" Her eyes widened. "You mean, you risk your life all the time?"

"No. Well, I used to. Now, I just—I take on jobs nobody else wants. My brothers and I—"

"You have brothers?"

"Two. We're close. Matt, Alex and I were in the service together. Then we—we worked for a government agency."

She was right, he was a warrior. "The FBI?"

"Nothing that aboveboard. Nothing with initials you'd recognize." His tone roughened. "I did things… We all did."

"Dangerous things."

"Yes, but—"

"For your country."

"Well, sure, but—"

"Someone has to do those things," she said softly. "For the rest of us, Cameron."

He looked down into her eyes. She meant every word. It was what he had believed, too, at first. Hell, he still believed it; in his heart, he knew it was true.

It was just that you grew tired of it all. The deceit. The tricks. The house of cards you built and tried to live in until it fell down around your ears.

"Yeah," he said gruffly. "But after a while, you start to forget that. We all did, Matt and Alex and me. That was when we knew it was time to get out. So we went home—"

"To Dallas."

"Right. And we formed Knight, Knight and Knight. Risk Management Specialists."

Leanna smiled. "Meaning, you're still in love with excitement."

He always had been. Now, all the excitement he'd ever need was right here, in his arms.

"My very own knight in shining armor," she said, laughing up at him. She caught his face between her palms, stood on her toes and kissed him. "How did I get lucky enough to find you in Baslaam?"

Cam caught her hands and brought them to his chest. "Long story," he said. "The bottom line is that I was there on business, for my father."

"Then, why did Asaad want me to—to distract you? Why did he want to hurt you?"

"What he wanted was my signature on a contract, but he knew I wouldn't sign. Maybe he figured if he grabbed me when I was—" He managed a quick smile. "When I was distracted, I'd have been easier to handle. His men would have worked me over, then made it clear they were going to—to do things to you, unless I cooperated."

Leanna didn't have to ask what things they'd have done. Instead she concentrated on what Cam had said about cooperation.

"And, once you did… He'd have killed you. And amused himself with me."

Her voice trailed away. Cam shut his eyes, trying to block out the rage that swept through him, knowing she needed words of reassurance and not crazed vows to kill Asaad with his bare hands.

"Don't be afraid, Salome. He'll never touch you. I swear it."

Leanna lifted her face to his. In the darkness, his torso naked, he looked like the fierce, proud soldier that he was.

"How can I be afraid of anything," she said softly, "when I'm in your arms?"

Her words were like a knife to his heart. He'd made her a vow that was less a promise than a prayer. Lots could go wrong and if they did, he had only one way of saving her from the sultan.

He didn't want to think about that.

What he wanted was to carry her back to the bed, make love to her until she forgot everything but him. Because what he felt for her was—it was—

"Cam? I want to—to thank you for what you did before." She blushed. "In the bath. It was—it was very generous."

Generous? She made it sound like a charity contribution.

"It was gallant."

The last thing he felt was gallant. His body was on fire.

"That's why I've decided to sleep on the sofa."

He blinked. "You what?"

"The sofa in the sitting room. I'm going to sleep on—"

"You are not."

"Of course I am. I know why you left the bed. I'm not a fool."

"I left it because I woke up and wanted a drink of water."

"You left because of me. That's the reason I'm going to sleep on—"

"What are you talking about?" First she talked about

wanting him, then she called him gallant. Now she was
hinting that he lacked self-control. It wasn't true. He had
loads of self-control, damn it. Buckets of it. "You're
sleeping in that bed, with me."

"I am not. You need your rest."

"I'll decide what I need. And watch how you speak
to me, Salome. I'm only going to take just so much before I lose my patience."

"Good night, Cameron."

Each time she called him that, his temperature went
up another five degrees.

"My name," he said testily, "is Cam."

"Sleep well."

"Salome. Salome, don't you dare turn your back and
walk away."

He watched, openmouthed, as she marched away
from him, the robe swinging loose on her shoulders, her
posture that of a queen who'd just dismissed one of her
subjects. What in hell had just happened? One minute,
she was in his arms, sweet and sexy as a man could
want; the next, she was all but patting him on the head
and telling him to be sure and take his vitamins.

"Damn it," he shouted, "you think you're the only
one having trouble with this?"

"I'm not having trouble with anything. You did that
generous thing for me when we were in the tub, and—"

Taut with anger, he went after her, clamped a hand
on her shoulder and spun her toward him.

"Do not walk away from me, woman!"

"Please. Calm down, Cameron."

"Do I look like a generous man to you? Do I?"

"It was a compliment."

"Well, I don't want that kind of compliment," he snarled, even though a little voice inside was assuring him he was behaving like a fool. "Compliments are the last thing I want from you."

"Really?"

"You're damned right, really."

Her smile was as old as Eve. "Then, what do you want from me, Cameron?" she said.

And he knew that he'd been scammed.

"Witch," he said softly.

She smiled. Rose on her toes. Laced her arms around his neck and opened her mouth to the wicked thrust of his tongue as he lifted her from the floor and carried her through the dark rooms, to their bed.

"I'm not going to stop this time," he whispered.

"Don't stop. Don't ever stop. Don't—"

Cam tugged at his jeans, kicked them aside. He gathered his golden dancer into his arms and kissed her again and again, one kiss merging into the next.

This, he thought, this was what a man searched for his entire life, what *he'd* searched for without knowing it.

Leanna clasped his face, brought his mouth to hers. She was parched for his kisses. How had she lived without them all these years?

"Touch me," she whispered, arching toward him, wrapping her long legs around his hips. Her mons brushed against his erection and he groaned, gritted his teeth, felt the electric shock of that whispered caress shoot through his blood.

Hold on, he told himself, *hold back.*

This was her first time. He was ready. God, he was

more than ready, but he had some control left. Not much, but enough to know he wanted it to be right. To be everything for her.

She sighed. Arched against him again, and he was lost.

A growl rumbled in his throat. He bent his head, sucked first one sweet nipple and then the other into his mouth. Rolled his tongue around them until she cried out and bucked with passion.

Then he moved lower, kissed and nipped his way down her rib cage, dipped his tongue into her navel.

Brushed his mouth over the golden curls at the junction of her thighs.

"No," she said, "Cam—"

"Yes," he said, catching her hands as she tried to push him away, lifting her arms, pinning her hands above her head. "Yes," he said thickly, and nuzzled against those soft curls, parting her labia, exposing the heart of her desire to his eyes and mouth.

Slowly he tongued her clitoris. Inhaled her woman's scent. Tongued her again and again until a wild cry burst from her throat.

He looked up, saw her head thrashing against the silken pillows. He let go of her wrists, slid his hands under her buttocks, lifted her to him and tasted her again.

"Please," she sobbed, her eyes blind with need, her hands clutching at his shoulders, "oh, please…"

He entered her. Slowly. God, yes. Slowly, even though his heart was pounding. Her lips formed his name and he leaned down, kissed her mouth, let her taste her own passion on her lips.

He wasn't going to be able to hang on much longer. The tightness of her vaginal muscles adjusting to his size, the little cries of pleasure rising from her throat, the taste of her mouth…

She whispered his name as he pressed forward.

"Am I hurting you?" he said. "I don't want to hurt—"

She moved. Moved again, and he knew there was no turning back.

In one quick motion, Cam broke through the fragile barrier that had protected his Salome's innocence. She gasped; her eyes widened and he forced himself to hold still, waiting, watching until he saw what he'd longed to see in her face.

Radiance.

Joy.

Everything that was unfolding in his own heart.

"Salome. My Salome…"

"Yes," she said, "oh, yes."

He could feel the rush of pure energy building inside him.

"Now," he said, and as she cried out in ecstasy, Cam threw back his head and exploded deep, deep within her golden heat.

CHAPTER TEN

AT THE first pale light of dawn, Leanna opened her eyes and found Cam watching her, his expression so tender it made her heart skip a beat.

"Good morning, sweetheart." He gave her a gentle kiss. "Did you sleep well?"

"Mmm-hmm." She cupped his cheek with her hand; he turned his face against it and kissed her palm. "You?"

He had hardly closed his eyes, trying to come up with a way to save them. Still, to his surprise, he felt rested.

Maybe it had to do with holding Salome in his arms as she slept.

"I'm fine." Carefully he drew her close. "Are you all right? I mean… Did I hurt you? I tried not to, but—"

Smiling, she laid her fingers across his lips. "It was wonderful, Cam. I never dreamed making love would be so—so—"

"Incredible," he said softly. "I know. For me, too." He drew her closer and buried his face against her throat. After a minute, he lifted his head and looked at her. "I'm glad we had that quarrel."

"What quarrel?" she asked, but the pink flush that rose in her cheeks told him she knew exactly what he meant.

"The one you provoked that was bound to lead to trouble."

Her laugh was soft and sexy. "Is this trouble?" she whispered as she ran her hands lightly down his back.

"Keep it up," he said, smiling, "and it will be."

"What a lovely promise."

Cam kissed her again. Her mouth was early-morning sweet, her skin carried the scent of their lovemaking. He cupped her breast, lowered his lips to the tip and played his tongue over it.

Salome closed her eyes. A sweet moan trembled in her throat.

He had made love to her again during the night, taking her slowly, lingering over the secrets of her body, but time was becoming their enemy.

"Sweetheart." Cam paused. "We have to get up."

Her sigh of acceptance whispered against his throat. "I know."

"We'll try the cell phone," he said, hoping he sounded as if he had every confidence he'd have better luck today than last night. "And I want to question Shalla. There has to be some kind of transportation here that I just haven't seen. A car. A truck. Something."

"I just wish…"

"Yes?"

"I wish," she said softly, "oh, I wish…"

"I know," he said, and despite all his good intentions, he drew her into his arms and kissed her again, his kisses deepening, his body quickening as she responded to him.

"Cameron," she whispered breathlessly, and he forgot everything but this, the feel of her as he guided her over him, the heat of her as he brought her down onto his erection, the look on her face as he filled her.

"Salome," he said, and she shuddered, flung back her head and rode him until the universe shattered.

A servant girl, eyes downcast, brought them clothes.

"My mistress wishes to know if you would like to take breakfast in the garden."

Cam said they would, and she bowed her way out.

They bathed, and diligently kept their hands off each other. Then they dressed. White linen trousers and a matching silk sweater for Leanna, chinos and a white T-shirt for Cam. There were leather sandals for them both.

His Salome looked beautiful in the new outfit, so beautiful that it was hard to leave the little world they'd created, but Cam knew they had to.

He knelt beside the bed, felt underneath it for the gun he'd stashed between the mattress and the springs. Leanna watched him tuck it into his waistband, then pull his shirt down over it.

"Do you think—do you think something's going to happen this morning?"

"What I think," he said quietly, "is that it's best to be prepared." He hesitated. "Why don't I go downstairs, have a little talk with our hostess, check things out and then you can join me for… What's the matter?"

"You're not going downstairs without me."

He decided not to argue. Until he knew more, he'd feel better keeping his Salome close. Not that he'd be much protection to her if Asaad's men stormed the palace, but he had a gun.

He'd use it against the enemy…and use it to keep

Salome from falling into the sultan's vicious hands, if it came to that.

What he was thinking must have shown in his face because she came close to him and put her arms around him.

"No matter what happens," she whispered, "I want to be with you."

"Sweetheart." Cam cleared his throat. "If things should go bad—if there's no way out—"

She drew his head down to hers and kissed him. "I know," she whispered, and when he looked into her eyes, he realized that she did.

They ate on the terrace, under a clear blue sky. A lattice-work of vines arched over their heads, shielding them from the sun. Birds fluttered in the trees, and brilliantly hued butterflies swooped over a bed of pale pink roses.

Shalla appeared while they were having their coffee. Was everything to their liking? The food, the clothes? She sounded like the friendly proprietor of an upscale B and B, Cam thought, and admitted to himself what he'd known all along.

He didn't trust her.

All the more reason to phrase his question carefully.

"I don't see any vehicles," he said. "Surely there must be some."

"Vehicles?"

"Yes. Trucks. Cars." When she looked at him blankly, his voice hardened. "Something that brings in supplies."

"Ah. We are self-sufficient here, my lord. We grow our own food, shear our own sheep. Everything you see was made by us."

The silk and linen clothing? The ornate furnishings?

The exotic foods? Cam wasn't buying it but he knew better than to call Shalla a liar to her face.

"Very impressive, but who is 'us'? I haven't seen anyone except you and one servant."

"Oh, there are others in the village."

The village. For the first time, he felt a stir of hope. "Where is this village?"

"It is not far, sir."

"Surely there must be some sort of transportation there?"

"A few wagons and mules, that is all."

Wagons and mules against a fleet of Humvees. Still, that was something. They'd make better time than if they walked. Besides, Cam had lifted Salome's feet to his lips for kisses when they made love this morning. The toes on one foot were red and swollen. When he'd asked about it, she'd brushed his question aside.

"My feet are the toughest part of me," she'd said. "Dancers get used to a little pain. Sometimes, we go off-stage with blood in our shoes." She'd laughed at his shocked expression. "We only look fragile, Cameron. It's part of the illusion."

A wagon it would be, he thought, and smiled politely at Shalla.

"In that case, I'd like to visit your village as soon as possible."

A look swept over her face. It was fleeting but it set off a warning bell in his head. The sooner they got that wagon and a couple of mules, the better.

"Of course, sir. I have some chores to attend to first. I will take you when the sun is high over the palace. Is that suitable?"

The whole damned situation wasn't suitable, but what could he do to change it?

"It's fine," Cam said briskly. "Just fine."

Leanna waited until Shalla was gone. Then she leaned close to Cam.

"Wagons and mules? That's all they have?"

"So the lady claims."

"Do you believe her?"

"What I believe," he said carefully, "is that wagons and mules are all we're going to get. Hey, look at the bright side. We won't have to worry about finding gas stations." She smiled up at him and he wrapped his arm around her. "One way or another, I'll do whatever it takes to get you home."

"To get both of us home," she said, her eyes locked to his. "I don't want to go home unless it's with you, Cameron. Do you understand?"

He saw the expression in her eyes and he knew what she was telling him.

She thought she'd fallen in love with him.

He knew better.

What she felt, what he felt, was a wild blur of sexual passion and danger, heightened for her because he was her first lover; heightened for him because—because…

Because she was special.

But it wasn't love.

He didn't believe in love. Not that kind. He loved his country. His brothers. The men who'd fought and bled beside him. But the June-moon thing was the creation of cheap songs and bad movies. People who let themselves believe it existed left themselves weak and vulnerable.

Why else would his mother have tolerated his father's coldness? His constant disapproval?

Why else would she have succumbed to illness and died?

No, Cam didn't believe in love. In the power of sex, yes. Add danger to the mix and you had a potent brew. A memorable one. He didn't love Salome and she didn't love him. She only thought she did and he—he only thought—he only thought—

To hell with what he thought.

Cam slipped his hands into his dancer's hair and lifted her face to his. Then he kissed her, slowly, telling her with his kiss that he would protect her with his life.

Honor was an emotion he understood.

"It's going to be okay, sweetheart."

"Is it possible… Could Asaad have given up looking for us?"

Given up? No way. Despite overwhelming odds, two people had escaped from Baslaam. They'd outwitted a small, well-equipped army. Instead of a contract worth millions, Asaad had suffered a humiliating loss of face.

Still, a little hope never hurt.

"Anything's possible," he said gruffly.

Leanna sighed and leaned against him. His arms tightened around her until she couldn't tell where her heartbeat ended and his began.

"Yes," she said quietly. "Anything's possible."

Cam kissed her. For another little while, they could go on living in a dream.

They tried the cell phone half a dozen times. From the front steps, from the garden, and, finally, from beside the pool.

No success. The phone couldn't pick up a signal.

"They never work when you want them to," Leanna said. She'd meant to sound matter-of-fact. Instead she suspected she'd sounded defeated. "Maybe later. Maybe whatever satellite it uses isn't in the right position. Maybe—"

Cam reached for her hand and drew her down onto the soft grass.

"There's no sense worrying about it, Salome. Another hour, Shalla will take me to the village and—"

"Us," Salome said. "She'll take us to the village."

"No." Gently he laid her back on the grass. "I'm going by myself."

"Suppose it's a trap. Suppose Asaad's men are waiting in that village."

"Suppose you do as I say for a change," he said, softening the words with a smile. "I want you to stay here with the door bolted and the gun beside you."

"You can't go without a gun. I won't let you."

"I can think of better things to do than quarrel."

"You're just trying to change the subject."

"Clever woman."

"Cam. If—if something should happen—"

"Nothing will."

He sounded positive, but she knew it was for her sake. "I know…but if something should—"

She squealed as he rolled her beneath him. "Have you always been such a pushy broad?"

Leanna laughed. "Yes."

Cam smiled and tweaked the end of her nose. "Tell me."

"Tell you what?"

"Tell me about you."

"The story of my life, you mean? Okay, but I get to ask you a question first."

"Yeah?"

"Yeah." She pushed up the sleeve of his T-shirt and danced her fingertips over the eagle on his bicep. "Tell me about this."

To her delight, he blushed. "It's just a silly tattoo."

"It's a spectacular tattoo."

"You think?" He grinned. "Well, that's good because my brothers and I think so, too. See, we were born a year apart, so I graduated from high school first. The night before I left for college, we realized it was the first time we were going to be separated."

"So you all got the same tattoo?"

"Yeah. Kid stuff, you know, but then—"

"Then, it became a bond between you. My brothers would think it was cool."

"Are they dancers, too?"

"My brothers?" Leanna snorted, then erupted in laughter. "Ohmygod, if they ever heard you say that…"

"No, huh?" he said, laughing with her. He loved her laugh. It was natural, just like her.

"They're police officers. Cops. Swat-team guys. They'd beat you up if you called them dancers. Well, no. They probably wouldn't be able to beat you up. I mean, they're big, like you. But—"

"But, they'd try."

"Absolutely. They still tease me about 'the dahnce,'" she said, raising her eyebrows, "whenever they can."

Cam plucked a daisy and ran the petals lightly over her mouth.

"They laugh, but I bet they're proud as hell of you."

"They are now." She grinned. "Of course, it was different when I first began dancing. I was six and we performed *The Nutcracker*—do you know what that is?"

"Trust me," Cam said dryly, "we have culture as well as barbecue in Texas."

"Well, my whole family came to watch, except I didn't tell them in advance that I was dancing the part of—"

"The Sugar Plum Fairy?"

"A doll under the Christmas tree. Meaning, I just sat slumped over and never, ever moved. Oh, I was devastated! I decided to switch from ballet to tap."

"Ballet's loss."

"Well, no. Because actually—"

"Actually, you're a wonderful dancer." Cam waggled his eyebrows. "That dance you did for me last night, for example…"

She blushed. "I don't want to talk about that."

"I do. Man oh man, when I looked up and saw you…"

"I've never danced like that before. A girl I knew in Vegas tried to convince me to try out for the show she was in but I just couldn't see myself, you know, doing a—a—"

"A strip," Cam said, and grinned when she blushed again. "And a good thing." His tone was teasing, but his eyes had a dangerous glint. "Because if I thought any other guy had seen you like that, I'd have to kill him."

His words thrilled her. What on earth had become of her feminist soul? "You're very protective."

"Yes," he said bluntly. "Is that bad?"

"No. Oh, no. I love the way you make me feel. As if—as if you—you really—"

"As if I really what?"

Leanna stared up into his eyes. *As if you really love me,* she thought…but she knew it wasn't true. Cam was her lover, not the man who loved her.

"As if you can do anything you set your mind to," she said.

Cam's smile tilted. "I hope that's true. I hope to hell I can get us out of this, Salome."

He kissed her. A long, deep kiss that almost made her die with the pleasure of it.

"Cam?" she whispered against his mouth. "Let's go upstairs."

His body hardened in instant response.

"Let's," he said softly.

Rising, he swept her into his arms, and carried her to their sanctuary.

He undressed her slowly, loving the passion in her face, in his blood. He stroked her, kissed her, brought her to the point where she could do nothing except sob his name. Then he took off his own clothes and carried her to the mirrored wall in the bedroom.

"Look at how beautiful you are, sweetheart," he whispered, turning her toward the glass. "God, look at you!"

Leanna looked.

Cam had taken her virginity, made love to her, bathed her. He'd kissed every inch of her; nothing about her body was a secret to him anymore. She thought he'd shared every experience with her.

Now, she knew he hadn't. Seeing yourself reflected in your lover's eyes wasn't the same as looking into a mirror as he made love to you.

His hands rose, cupped her breasts. She gasped at the

rush of sensation, the liquid heat that gathered low in her belly as she saw his thumbs move over her nipples.

"Watch," he whispered.

She couldn't have torn her gaze from the mirror if she'd tried.

One of his hands still cupped her breast. The other followed the curve of her waist, her hip, slowly spread over her belly in a gesture so erotically possessive it made her knees buckle.

"Cam," she said in a choked voice.

She felt his mouth at her nape, his teeth against her skin.

"Watch," he said again, his voice rough with command.

He slid his hand between her thighs. She gasped; her body wept warm tears against his palm, then arched like a bow as the shock of her orgasm transformed her into a quicksilver flash of light.

She had come in his arms each time they'd made love, but never like this. Cam turned her toward him and held her tight, wanting the moment to last forever.

"Cam," she said in wonder, "oh God, Cam…"

He cupped her bottom, lifted her to him and slipped deep inside her. Leanna gave a ragged cry and locked her legs around his waist as he filled her. Deeper. Deeper. Only his strength, his embrace, his erection kept her from collapsing to the floor.

They came together in an explosive burst of energy. Leanna wept unashamedly; Cam cried out. He drew her down to the floor and held her tightly against his thundering heart.

Something was happening to him, something he didn't understand or want or…

An unearthly roar filled the air. The windows shattered and Leanna screamed in terror. Cam flung his body over hers as glass flew into the room.

Outside the window, an enormous black helicopter hovered over the garden, its bulk blocking out the sky.

CHAPTER ELEVEN

"CAM," Leanna screamed, "Cam, what's happening?"

He rolled away from her, grabbed his trousers and pulled them on. The 'copter had moved out of view and was descending. He could hear the *whap-whap* of its blades.

"They found us, sweetheart."

"The sultan's men? But—but Shalla said this place was a sanctuary."

"Shalla lied." Glass was in his hair. He could feel tiny shards of it under his feet but he was okay except for that. He grabbed Salome, looked her over quickly, breathed a little easier once he was convinced she wasn't hurt.

"Get dressed."

She grabbed her clothes, yanked them on with shaking hands. Cam picked up the gun, jacked a shell into the chamber and headed for the door.

Leanna ran after him. "Cam, wait!"

He swung toward her, bare-chested, barefoot, the gun in his hand.

"Bolt the door after me."

"No! I'm going with you!"

"Bolt it and don't open it, no matter what you hear. Not unless I tell you to open it."

"Cameron. I'm not letting you go out there alone."

"You damned well are."

Leanna stared at Cam. For a moment, he looked like a dangerous stranger. But he wasn't. He was the man she loved.

Whatever happened, she wanted to be with him, even if it meant dying with him.

"I'm going with you, Cam. You can't stop me."

"Damn it, Salome, I don't have time to argue!"

"That's right. You don't. So get used to it. I'm going—"

He grabbed her by the shoulders. "The hell you are!"

Men were shouting and yelling in the distance. He had to get down the stairs, let himself be seen. Run. Lead the bastards away from her and take out as many as he could.

All he had were minutes to try and save his golden dancer. And if he couldn't—if he couldn't, he'd keep one bullet. For her. A quick, painless death would be all he could give her to remember him by through eternity.

"Salome. Salome, sweetheart—"

"Don't 'sweetheart' me! I'm not letting you go out there alone."

She meant it. He could see that glint in her eye, that tilt to her chin. The determination that was part of who she was, but he'd be damned if that would do her any good this time.

No way would he take her with him. He was trained in survival. He could deal with what waited outside this door. She would be at the mercy of the killers who'd come for them.

"I'm done arguing," he said bluntly. "You're staying here."

"Please." Her voice broke. She put her hands on his chest and looked up at him, tears bright in her eyes. "I know you're trying to protect me. And—and I love you for it. I love you for everything you are, Cam. Do you hear me? I love you!"

There they were, the words he'd known she wanted to say, the words he knew couldn't really be true.

Then, why did they pierce his heart?

"That's why you have to let me go with you," she said. "Don't you see? I love you!"

He had to silence her. Had to force her to stay behind. There was only one way to do it, even if it hurt her.

Cam took her hands from his chest and yanked them to her sides. "Don't be a child," he said sharply. "We had sex, lady. Sex. Don't confuse it with love."

She blanched. "You're wrong. I love you."

"And I love breathing," he said, hating himself more than he'd ever thought possible. This wasn't the way their affair was supposed to end, but he'd run out of choices. Saving her was all that mattered. His honor demanded it. "I'm going outside. You're staying here until I get back. You got that?"

Her face was white. Her mouth trembled. He cursed, drew her to him and crushed her mouth with his. She didn't respond and he could have sworn he felt his soul shatter as he let her go.

"Remember to throw the bolt."

Then he went out the door, waited until he heard the lock slide home and raced down the stairs.

The sultan's thugs were in the courtyard. Six men.

No, eight. Cam felt the old, familiar surge of adrenaline. One last deep breath. Then he gave a rebel yell and started moving, firing as he ran.

Two men went down. A third, then a fourth. Cam raced for the side of the building, bullets whining past his head. He turned the corner and flattened himself against the wall. For the first time, he let himself think he and Salome might just survive this…except, there were more men coming, crouched low as they raced toward him.

Too many men. Too many guns.

This was it, then. He was outnumbered and outgunned. It was time to get back to Salome. Hold her in his arms. Tell her that these few days had been—that they had been wonderful. Kiss her mouth, put the gun to her temple…

Something hit him in the chest.

It felt like a sledgehammer. But why would anybody be wielding a sledge—a sledge—

"Ahhh."

Pain blossomed like a multi-petaled flower, radiating through his chest, his shoulders, his arms. Cam slid down the wall. He looked down, touched his chest, came away with smears of crimson on his fingers.

The sound of gunfire faded. A boot kicked at his leg. He raised his eyes, saw a man standing over him. It was hard to see clearly—things had become hazy, for some reason—but he knew that cruel face.

"Asaad?"

"Mr. Knight." A delighted smile. Another prod of the boot. "How nice to see you again."

Cam grunted and tried to struggle to his feet. The sultan laughed, jammed his foot on Cam's chest and pushed him back.

"I'm afraid you won't be going anywhere, Mr. Knight. Did you really think you could escape me?"

Salome. Where was she? Cam had to get to her.

"Are you looking for someone? Of course you are. You're looking for my harem girl."

Cam labored for breath. "Not yours," he wheezed. "Never—"

Asaad jerked his head to the side and barked a command. One of his men came forward, dragging something—someone—behind him.

Cam's eyes filled with tears.

It was his Salome. A rope was looped around her neck; her hands were bound. Her face was dirty and bruised. And she was weeping.

"Cam," she sobbed. "Oh, Cam!"

Asaad watched, smiling. He let her get within inches of Cam. Then, still smiling, he grabbed her by the hair and yanked her back.

"I only regret that you will not live to watch me enjoy my prize, Mr. Knight. I suppose you won't live long enough to sign that oil lease, either, but it's almost worth the privilege of seeing you—"

Cam raised his gun. The sultan's eyes widened with shock.

"Bang," Cam whispered, and pulled the trigger.

A perfect hole appeared in the center of Asaad's forehead and he crumpled to the ground, lifeless.

Thwap. Thwap. Thwap.

One of the sultan's men let out a wild cry. Cam looked at Salome. *Now,* he told himself. *Now.* One bullet remained. One bullet to spare her agony.

God, no. He couldn't. Couldn't…

Thwap. Thwap. Thwap.

A giant bird dropped from the sky, a Blackhawk helicopter painted in desert camouflage. Shots rang out. Asaad's men scattered. Too late. They were easy targets.

Then there was silence, except for the sigh of the wind.

Cam struggled to lift his head. Tried to speak his golden dancer's name. Tried to go to her.

"Cameron? Cameron, goddammit, man, can't we take our eyes off you for a minute?"

Cam blinked. His vision was graying out, but he could have sworn he saw his brothers leaning over him.

"Damn it, Cam, keep your eyes open. Do not close your eyes. You hear that? You die on us, bro, we're never going to forgive you." Matt's voice was harsh but his hands were gentle.

"Get his head up," Alex said gruffly.

"Salome," Cam whispered.

Matt's head bent to his. "What?"

"Salome. My golden dancer…"

And then the gray turned black, and Cam fell into an ocean of darkness.

Noise. Lights. Pain, sharp as the blade of a knife. Pinpricks and a duller pain, pulsing with each beat of his heart.

Salome.

Salome.

And then, again, darkness.

Voices. Some that were familiar, some that weren't.

"Not good."

"…best we can, but—"

"…significant loss of blood."

"...young. Strong. No promise, but—"

And always, always, a single name inside his head. *Salome.*

And then, one morning, Cameron opened his eyes.

He was in a white-walled room. Lights traced irregular patterns on a monitor; something was beeping with annoying constancy. Plastic tubes snaked into his arms, and an invisible mastodon was camped on his chest.

Cam groaned.

He couldn't be dead. Even if he'd believed in heaven and hell, neither place would look like this.

The good news was that he was in a hospital bed.

The bad news was that he was in a hospital bed and not one of the faces grouped around him was Salome's.

"Hey, bro."

Cam turned his head a fraction of an inch. Alex flashed a wobbly grin.

"Glad you decided to stay around."

Cam tried to answer but he felt as if someone had scooped all the sand from the desert and dumped it down his throat.

"He wants water," someone else said. It was Matt, who reached out and gripped his shoulder. "Good to see you again," he said gruffly.

"Ice chips," another voice said authoritatively. "The nurse said no water, remember? Here, let me do it."

Cam blinked as his father eased a hand around his nape and gently supported him so he could reach a paper cup filled with ice.

His old man? Bending over him with damp eyes? Maybe he really was dead, after all. But the ice was real and wonderfully wet, and his father's mouth was curved in a smile.

"Welcome home, son. It's good to have you back."

Cam nodded. "Yeah," he rasped. "Iss good to be back." He took a long breath, trying not to wince at the sudden stab of pain in his chest. "Salome?"

His father's brow furrowed. His brothers looked at each other.

"Who?"

"Salome," he said impatiently. "My gldn'ncer."

"Ah. The woman." Alex nodded reassuringly. "She's fine. Not a scratch on her."

Cam closed his eyes, fought against the black water trying to close over his head.

"Wan'see her."

Another look passed between his brothers. "Sure," Matt said. "Soon as you're feeling better."

"Wan'seehernow," Cam said, and the room began to spin.

"Cameron," his father said, but his voice seemed to come from a long way off.

The darkness sucked him under.

He awoke a couple of more times, but it was always the same. His brothers, his father. Doctors, nurses, machines.

No Salome.

And then, finally, he swam up from the dark depths, opened his eyes and knew he was better. The mastodon on his chest had been replaced by an elephant. There was only one tube in his arm and the blinking, beeping machines were gone.

Cam turned his head. Looked around. His brothers were sprawled in a pair of too-small chairs near the window.

"Hey," he said.

What came out sounded like the croak of a sick frog but they heard him. They shot from their chairs, almost tripped over each other as they hurried to his side.

"Hey, yourself," Matt said.

Cam ran the tip of his tongue over his lips. "How long?"

"Two weeks," Alex replied.

Two weeks. God, two weeks!

"Salome?"

Matt made a *cluck-cluck* sound Cam knew meant he was stalling for time.

"What about this Salome?"

"I want to see her."

His brothers exchanged a quick look. "Well," Matt said cautiously, "you get back on your feet, I'm sure you'll be able to—"

"She's not here?"

"No," Alex said, "she's not."

Had he dreamed his brothers had told him she was safe? Cam struggled up against the pillows.

"Didn't you get her out with me? You did, didn't you? You didn't leave—"

"Easy, man. Of course we got her out. Took her on the chopper." Alex squeezed Cam's hand. "Landed you on board the *USS Sentry*. You were hanging on by a thread. You needed medical attention, fast."

"What happened to Salome?"

"The chopper took her to Dubai."

"And?"

"And…" Alex blew out a breath. "After that, I don't know."

"What do you mean, you don't know?"

"He means," Matt said carefully, "we don't know. We stayed beside you on the *Sentry* while the medics worked on you. When you were stabilized, they air-lifted you out."

"You never checked to see what had happened to Salome in Dubai?"

"No," Alex said bluntly, "we didn't. It never occurred to us. We were too busy making sure you didn't do something stupid, like die."

Cam looked at his brothers. Their eyes reflected what they'd gone through over the last weeks.

"Yeah," he said softly. "Right." He managed a quick smile. "One of us never could get away from the others, I guess."

"Damned right," Matt said. "Even the old man stuck to you like glue."

Cam nodded. "Yeah." His voice roughened. "Thanks. For everything. I mean, for a while there, I kind of figured I'd imagined seeing you ugly so-and-so's climbing out of that big, beautiful bird." He paused. "Asaad? Did I really get him?"

"The son of a bitch is history. You would have been, too, if that call you made on your cell hadn't gotten through. We got just enough info to figure out your location."

"And save my life."

"Yup. Us and a few pals from the old days saved your sorry ass, and don't think we're gonna let you forget it."

The brothers grinned at each other. Then Cam ran his tongue over his lips.

"She phoned, right? Salome?" There was an uncomfortable silence. "Phoned you? To find out how I was doing?"

"Actually…actually, no. Not me," Alex said. "Matt? You hear anything?"

"Sorry, man. She hasn't been in touch."

"But—but—" *But, why would she call? He'd said things meant to hurt her. Or—or maybe she couldn't call. Maybe she'd never gotten to Dubai.*

"Cam?"

"Yeah." Cam cleared his throat. "I have to find out what happened to her."

"Okay." Matt reached for a notepad and pencil. "Give me her name and address, and I'll—"

"I don't know it."

"Just her name, then, and her town… What?"

"I told you, I don't know."

"The town?"

"Any of it. Where she lives, where she's from." A muscle knotted in Cam's jaw. "I don't even know her name."

His brothers stared at him as if he'd lost his mind. He couldn't blame them. How could he have spent those days and nights with Salome and never once asked her her name?

"It isn't Salome?" Alex said.

Cam gave a bitter laugh. "I'm the one who came up with that."

Matt frowned. "You don't know this babe's name?"

"Don't call her that," Cam said tightly.

"What am I supposed to call her, then? Salome?"

"No," Cam said roughly. "I'm the only one who can

call her…" He fell silent. "I've got to find her," he said, and from the way he said it, his brothers knew he was right.

Salome had vanished. It was as if she'd never existed, except in Cam's dreams.

He demanded to have a phone plugged in beside his bed.

His doctors objected. He needed rest. Cam said he knew what he needed a lot better than they did and after the nurses found him all but crawling down the hall to a public telephone, his doctors threw up their hands and said yes, fine, he could have a bedside phone.

Not that it helped.

He phoned the American consul in Dubai. The consul was on vacation and his clerk said she'd love to be of help but did Mr. Knight have any idea how many Americans traipsed in and out of the embassy every week?

"The thing is, sir…" Thousands of miles separated Cam and the clerk, but Cam could almost see the woman's raised eyebrows. "If you knew the lady's name…"

"I don't," Cam snapped.

"Are you sure she came to the embassy?"

Cam had to admit that he wasn't. Salome was without her passport but that didn't necessarily mean she'd have gone to the embassy. Maybe she'd just called someone. Someone in her dance troupe. Someone who was still in the place where she'd been kidnapped.

And he didn't know the name of the troupe, didn't know where she'd been when she was taken.

Damn it to hell, he didn't know anything!

I love you, she'd said.

Yeah, but if she loved him, she'd have come to him. Phoned. Damn it, she knew his name, knew he was from Dallas. She could have found him in a heartbeat. Why hadn't she?

Because you were right, a voice inside him said coldly. *It was sex and danger gave her that high, not you.*

Cam clenched his fists and stared at the ceiling over his hospital bed.

It that was true, fine. He'd known it all along. But he'd saved her life. Didn't she even want to find out if he'd lived or died?

She doesn't owe you a thing, Knight, the voice said, even more coldly.

She didn't. She didn't. She—

The hell she didn't. He had the right to see her one last time, hear her admit that what she'd thought she felt for him had evaporated as soon as she'd reached safety.

Then he could forget all about her.

The doctors said he'd be hospitalized another couple of weeks. He had to build his strength. Eat the baby-slop they served him, get up with an aide's help and walk the hall for fifteen minutes, three times a day. Then, the doctors added, then, maybe he could go home, move in with Matt or Alex or his father for a while.

"Right," Cam said, and made his own plans.

He phoned out for his meals. Steak. Pasta. Protein and carbs. He got up on his own every hour, walked for twenty minutes, then forty, then got out of bed and stayed out. A day later, he asked for his clothes, changed the polite request to a demand when a nurse tried to bully him with what she said was a rule about wearing hospital garments that left a man walking around with his ass hanging out.

He was standing at the window wearing jeans, sneakers and a sweatshirt when the pulmonologist who'd treated his collapsed lung and the thoracic surgeon who'd removed the bullet that had missed his heart by an eighth of an inch showed up.

"Being up and dressed makes me feel human again," he said, and waited for one of them to have the balls to ask if he'd confirmed that by looking in a mirror.

Later that afternoon, Cam checked himself out and went to the Turtle Creek condo he called home.

He was done wasting precious time. The longer it took him to start looking for Salome, the longer it would take to find her.

He was entitled to answers, damn it. And he was going to get them.

He flew to Dubai but he learned nothing. He flew home angrier than before, angry at the world, at Salome, at himself for giving a damn.

He contacted a private investigator who handled work for the firm and told him all he knew. Salome was a dancer. What kind? He ran their conversations through his mind. She'd talked about Las Vegas. About tap dancing. The P.I. nodded and made notes. Oh, and she had three brothers who were cops. The P.I. nodded, as if that really was useful information, and made more notes.

"A picture would help," the P.I. said, and arranged for Cam to meet with a woman do did sketches for the police. Three hours later, they had a passable drawing of Salome.

The P.I. ran off a few hundred copies and left for Vegas. Cam gave it a little thought and got on the next plane. Duplication of effort, the P.I. said, but so what? Cam trudged from hotel to hotel, club to club. Nothing. Nobody recognized the sketch; nobody knew Salome.

Home again in Dallas one Friday night, his brothers dragged him to the bar they frequented. He knew they wanted to talk, so he let them do it.

Matthew and Alexander hemmed and hawed and waltzed around the question of why Cam was so desperate to find a woman whose name he didn't know, who hadn't made any effort to find him, but Matt finally asked the question.

"So," he said carefully, "she's important to you, huh? This—uh, this woman, I mean."

"I want to know what happened to her." Cam's eyes narrowed. "You got a problem with that?"

"No problem," Matt said quickly.

"Yeah." Cam let out a breath. "Sorry. I'm just—"

"Edgy," Alex said. "Anybody would be, after all you've been through." He cleared his throat. "What I don't get," he said carefully, "is how a man gets involved with a ba— with a woman and never gets around to learning her name."

Cam thought about telling him it was none of his business, but he knew his brothers meant well. They loved him. They were just trying to figure out what in hell was going on.

So was he.

"We were on the run," he said. "It was a life-or-death situation. I gave her a nickname and it stuck."

"Salome," Alex said, shooting a sideways glance at Matt.

"Like the dancer who got the guy's head on a platter," Matt said.

"Which she could do without any sweat because she'd seduced him."

"You want to say something, just say it."

"Take it easy, man. We love you, that's all. We're worried about you. You took a bullet, lost a lot of blood, almost died—"

"And your point is?" Cam said, trying to lighten things and succeeding, at least for a few seconds, when all three of them laughed.

"Only what you already know," Alex said. "On the run, life or death… That tends to heighten things, you know?"

Cam nodded, picked up his beer, then put it down again.

"I told her that."

Alex nodded. "Good. I mean, it's good you understood that, because—"

"Of course I understood it. She was the one who didn't."

His brother gave relieved sighs. "You don't know how glad we are to hear you say that," Matt said, "because, you know, for a while there—"

Cam slammed his fist on the table.

"She lied, damn it! She said she loved me. Then, where the hell is she?"

"Yeah," Alex said cautiously, "but like you just said—"

"Nobody lies to me and gets away with it."

His brothers exchanged a baffled look. Cam had just said that this woman he called Salome hadn't really loved him. Then he'd said he wasn't going to let her get away with *not* really loving him.

Neither was foolish enough to point out that interesting inconsistency. Wise men that they were, they finished their drinks in silence.

Avery phoned late on a cold, miserable Saturday.

"How are you, son?"

Cam still wasn't used to the new tone in his father's voice, but he liked it. The old saying was true. Better late than never.

"I'm okay, Dad." He liked that, too. Thinking of Avery as "Dad."

"I haven't seen much of you lately."

"No. Well, I've been busy."

"I have one of those benefit things to attend tonight. I was hoping you might go with me."

"Thanks, Dad, but—"

"I thought we'd spend a little time together." Avery gave a laugh that was clearly forced. "It's an arts recital, Cameron. I can't get out of it but I can't imagine how I'm going to sit through it, either. With you there, you know, two cultural heathens side by side, I figure I might just make it."

It was so unlike anything his father had ever said to him that Cam felt his throat tighten.

"Your mother," Avery said with a little laugh. "Your mother used to love this stuff."

Cam held his breath. He couldn't recall his father ever mentioning his mother before.

"Did she?" he said carefully.

"She's the reason I began supporting these things. The Arts Council. The theater. The museum." Avery cleared his throat. "I don't know why, but I've been thinking about your mother a lot these past weeks.

How proud she'd be to see you and your brothers all grown up."

"Yes." Cam swallowed hard. "We—I—think about her, too."

"I loved her something fierce, Cameron." His father's voice grew husky. "So much that there were times I was afraid to show it. I know that sounds crazy, but—"

Unbidden, an image of Salome lying beneath him, her blue eyes dark with passion, flashed through Cam's mind. He shook it away, as a dog might shake water from its coat, just as his father spoke again.

"Well," Avery said briskly, "how about tonight? If you're not up for it, I'll understand."

"I'm up for it, Dad."

"Great, son. I'll pick you up at six-thirty."

Cam shaved. Showered. Put on his tux. Told himself that an evening out was a great idea. He wouldn't think about Salome. Not once—except to despise himself for thinking about her at all.

She was gone. Out of his life, and he couldn't have cared less.

Their seats in the baroque Music Hall were fourth row, center. Both men opened their programs.

"An Evening With The Arts," his father read aloud, and gave a deep sigh. "It's going to be endless, Cameron. A little of this, a little of that, none of it good. Speeches. Presentations. A soprano caterwauling, a boys' chorus trying to sound angelic. A flamenco guitarist and, good Lord, a *corps de ballet.* Thank you for coming, son. I'm eternally grateful."

Cam nodded. Somehow, he and his old man endured the first half. Went for drinks during intermission, said "hello" to lots of people though his father did less glad-handing than in the past. When the lights blinked, they returned to their seats.

Cam settled down next to his father. Smothered a yawn as an overweight lady trilled to an overweight guy in a bad toupee. Shifted his weight as another guy ruined what could have been a great bit on the guitar by trying to look dark and mysterious.

Polite applause for the guitarist. Rustles. Coughs. The curtains opened again; music softly swelled.

Cam folded his arms, watched from under his lashes as a group of ballerinas danced onstage.

"Got to admit, they're easy on the eyes," his father whispered…

And Cam damned near shot from his seat because the last ballerina tiptoeing out from the wings was Salome.

CHAPTER TWELVE

HE MUST have done something. Tensed up or maybe started to rise. Something, because his father clasped his arm and said, "Cameron?" in a low voice.

Cam sank back in his seat, staring at the stage where a dozen ballerinas whirled in graceful circles.

He had eyes for only one.

Her hair was drawn back in a demure chignon. She wore a lacy white thing—what was it called? A tutu. Right. Her ankles were crisscrossed by the white satin ribbons of her ballet shoes.

He felt his heart skip a beat.

Looking at her was like looking at a dream.

He could almost taste the sweetness of the tender skin beneath the chignon. See the perfection of her breasts hidden under the demure white lace. Hear the whisper of his name on her lips.

Oh, yes, it was his dancer. The packaging had changed but it was Salome, moving across the stage, arms raised in a graceful arc just as they'd been the night she'd danced for him in the moonlight.

The music was quick and bright. A waltz. One two three, one two three. His pulse kept time with it.

Look at me, he wanted to say. *Salome, look at me.*

But her eyes were demurely downcast, her head tilted at an angle that showed the creamy delicacy of her throat.

She wouldn't look up.

He couldn't look away.

Vegas, she'd said. Tap, she'd said. She'd never mentioned ballet or, yes, maybe she had, but only in passing. He started to smile. From this night on, he'd love ballet. It had brought her to him. She was here, she was fine…

Yes, she was here. In his city.

Cameron stiffened.

His city. And she hadn't come to him. Hadn't even called. She knew that he lived in Dallas. She knew his name, his profession and, goddammit, she hadn't even tried to find out if he'd survived.

"Cameron?"

His father leaned over, concern on his face. Cam figured he probably looked like a man who was about to explode. He was sitting rigidly in his seat, hands knotted into fists in his lap.

"Son, what's wrong? Are you feeling sick?"

He'd been right all along. It had been the excitement. The danger. She hadn't loved him, hadn't given a damn about him…

And that was fine. He didn't give a damn about her, either.

But he was furious. Enraged. All these weeks, he'd worried about what might have become of her but she—she—

"Son?"

"I'm fine, Dad. I just—I need some air, that's all."

Avery began to rise but Cam pressed him back in his seat. "Stay for the end. I'll meet you outside."

Cameron got to his feet. Worked his way to the aisle. Paused when he got there, looked at the stage but her head was turned away, eyes still fixed on the floor as she whirled toward the wings.

To hell with her, he thought coldly, and headed for the lobby.

He went for a late supper with Avery. Made small talk. Did whatever it took to convince the old man he was okay and no, he didn't need to phone the doctor.

When he figured enough time had passed, he pleaded a heavy workload the next morning and went home, where he paced his condo the first half of the night and spent the rest lying in bed, staring at the ceiling.

"Get over it," he said into the silence. "So she didn't come. Didn't call. So what?"

Actually he was lucky. Better to know she'd forgotten him in the blink of an eye than to have found himself dealing with a lovesick ballerina.

He went to his office in the morning, snarled at his secretary, at his brothers and finally grabbed his jacket, said he had an appointment and walked out. He got into his Porsche, gunned the engine and drove out of the city, drove aimlessly for what seemed forever until he pulled under a stand of aspens, got out of the car and walked along a rutted trail that wound down to a lake.

What kind of a woman was she? To give herself to a man, cry out in his arms, make him believe he was all she'd ever wanted in the entire world, even say she loved him, when it was all lies?

The adrenaline, remember? That's what it was. And, just in case there was any doubt, you gave her a dose of the real world. "We had sex, lady," you said. "Sex. Don't confuse it with love."

Cam kicked a stone aside.

Okay. Good. She'd never loved him. Hell, he never believed she had. But he'd saved her life…

For God's sake, man, are you back to that? That's pathetic. Besides, the life you were saving was your own. She just happened to be along for the ride.

No. Not true. At the end, his life hadn't mattered. Her life was all he'd cared about.

Damn it, he wanted answers!

Cam yanked his cell phone from his pocket. As usual, the miserable thing didn't work but this time all it took was a jog back to the road to make it light up like Broadway at night.

He punched in the P.I.'s number. Told him what he wanted. The name of a dancer with the ballet company performing at the Music Hall.

Could Mr. Knight narrow things down a bit? the P.I. asked. He had that sketch the police artist had done, but…

A day ago, Cameron would have identified Salome as the most beautiful woman in the world, but things had changed.

"She'll be simple to identify," he told the detective. "She's the only blonde. And I need to know where I can find her. She's got to be staying somewhere. An apartment. A hotel. I need the name."

"Fine, Mr. Knight. When do you need this information, sir?"

Cam narrowed his eyes. Hadn't the Music Hall's program said something about a limited run? For all he knew, tonight was Salome's last in Dallas.

"I needed it an hour ago," he said sharply.

The Porsche's tires screamed in protest as he put the car into a tight U-turn and headed for home.

The audience was still applauding. The *corps de ballet* was still onstage, but Leanna slipped away to the dressing room.

She couldn't wait to change into street clothes and get back to the hotel. One more night, and she'd leave Dallas behind.

Her hands shook as she tore the pins from her hair and shook it loose.

The week had been horrible, thinking about Cam all the time, seeing his face in every shadow.

And then last night—last night, she'd been sure he was in the theater. Crazy, of course, but she'd felt his presence, ridiculous as that sounded. Felt him looking at her.

She hadn't dared lift her head.

The company made only one brief appearance in this show, dancing a piece from *Swan Lake*.

"Eyes down," Nikolai had told them. During rehearsal, when one girl glanced up, he'd stomped and shouted that they were cows and if it happened again, he'd work them until they dropped.

They were all close enough to dropping as it was, Leanna especially, thanks to her stay in the hospital while she'd battled the infection in her foot. Dutifully she'd kept her eyes down as she'd danced.

Besides, if she'd looked up and seen Cam in the au-

*di*ence last night, she'd probably have—she'd proba-
bly have...

The truth was, she didn't know what she'd have done.

She'd almost lost her mind when she'd looked at the
company's schedule.

"Dallas?" she'd said to Ginny, who roomed with her
on the road. "Dallas?"

"Um," Ginny had replied. "Last-minute change in
plans."

"No," Leanna had said, trying to stay calm. "I can't
go to Dallas."

"Oh, it's a great city." Ginny had glanced up and
smiled. "Lots of terrific restaurants. Good shopping.
And, oh boy, the men..."

"I can't go there," Leanna had repeated.

Ginny's brows had lifted. "What's the problem?"

What, indeed? What could she have said that
wouldn't give everything away? Nobody knew about
her and Cam. Nobody needed to know. It was bad
enough she had to live with the memories of the time
they'd been together.

So she'd muttered some foolish excuse about being
in Texas before and hating the heat, and Ginny's brows
had shot up again.

"It's winter, Lee. It's gonna be cold in Dallas."

"Oh," Leanna had replied. "Oh, of course."

So she'd gone to Dallas. What choice did she have?
She needed her job. She was still amazed the company
had kept a spot open for her, after all the time she'd been
out, first because of the kidnapping and then because
she'd been ill.

She'd gone to Dallas, and lived through a week of hell.

Cam, she'd kept thinking, *Cam was here.*

How many times had she almost done something stupid? Too many to count, but she'd come close. Oh, so close! She'd looked up his name in the phone book. His home address wasn't listed but his firm was. Knight, Knight and Knight. Risk Management Specialists. Not that she'd do anything about it, she'd told herself...

But she'd taken a cab, gone to the address, stood staring at a tower of glass and steel while she came up with all the reasons it would be logical to just walk in and ask to see Cameron Knight.

After all, he'd saved her life.

Thank you, she'd say, *oh, and by the way, you were right, that stuff back on the other side of the world was just silliness.*

She hadn't done it.

She still had some pride left.

At least the week of torment was over. Tomorrow morning, she'd climb on the bus, close her eyes and when she opened them again, Dallas would be only a memory.

Like Cam.

Leanna dipped her fingers into a jar of cleansing cream and smeared it over her face.

There was no sense in thinking about him. She was back in the real world and so was he, and though she'd dreamed of it happening a thousand times, he'd made no attempt to get in touch with her but then, why would he?

He'd been brutally clear about what their relationship had meant to him. She knew he'd been deliberately blunt so she'd obey his orders, but the essence of what he'd said had been the unvarnished truth.

What had happened between them was a fairy tale, and fairy tales never lasted.

Leanna tissued off the cleansing cream.

She was sweaty and exhausted. Her muscles burned and even before she got her toe shoes unlaced, she knew she'd bled into them. That was one of the things that happened when you danced *en pointe*. Normally she didn't pay it much attention but after what had happened weeks ago, she knew enough to be cautious.

She'd collapsed in the chopper that took her to Dubai.

One second, she'd been weeping, incoherent even to herself, begging the men half-dragging her to the helicopter to let her go back to Cam. The next, the world went gray. She came to days later in a hospital bed, antibiotics pumping into her veins, an infection in her left foot and her temperature so high she was unconscious half the time.

When she finally surfaced, the first words she heard were the doctor's. He said she was a lucky young woman. She might have lost her foot—even died—after a couple more days without antibiotics.

The first words she spoke were about Cam. "Is he alive?" she'd whispered.

The doctor's shrug had been eloquent. He didn't know anything about someone named Cam.

She'd begged for word of Cam, but nobody knew what she was talking about. She had no phone. "No stress," the nurses told her, but finally she bribed an aide into smuggling in a cell phone. She called the embassy, fast-talked her way into being connected with the consul.

He was impatient. He was, he told her, leaving on vacation.

Leanna begged and pleaded and made such a pathetic case that he'd finally agreed to find out what he could about a man named Cameron Knight.

An hour later, he called back. Cameron Knight was alive. He'd been airlifted to the States. To a hospital in Dallas, Texas, and really, that was all he could tell her.

Leanna telephoned Dallas information, got the numbers of endless hospitals, called them all and finally found the right one. Yes, they had a patient named Cameron Knight. His condition was listed as stable. No, they couldn't tell her anything more than that.

She phoned each day, heard Cam's condition go from stable to satisfactory. She went on phoning after she was out of the hospital. She phoned from Paris, where she had a tearful reunion with the dance troupe. She phoned from London and from Seattle, after she began dancing again.

And then, one day, she phoned and got the operator who'd been taking most of her calls.

"Mr. Knight has been discharged," the woman said. "He's doing just fine." Then she'd lowered her voice and said, "You know, dear, you could find out more if you contacted the Knight family directly."

Contact the Knight family? And tell them what? That she'd slept with Cam? That she'd made a fool of herself, thinking she'd fallen in love with him? Because he was right, it hadn't been love, it had only been infatuation.

The dressing room door burst open and the other girls crowded in, laughing and chattering.

"Lee, you missed it all!" Ginny bounced onto the stool beside Leanna's. "The audience called us back three times!"

Leanna got up, stripped off her tutu and pulled on jeans and a sweater.

"I know. I could hear the cheers."

"And the most amazing thing just happened!" Ginny swung toward her, eyes bright with excitement. "A reporter wants to meet me!"

"Gin, that's wonderful."

"Isn't it? He says he's doing a piece on unusual professions for the Sunday section. I don't know how I got so lucky—I mean, to have him come up with my name—but I'm thrilled."

"I'll bet! But when's the interview? If we leave tomorrow—"

"He's taking me out for supper in—" Ginny looked at the big wall clock and gasped. "In ten minutes!"

"Then you'd better hurry," Leanna said, pulling her hair back in a ponytail.

Ginny peered into the mirror as she dabbed cream on her face. "I'll meet you at that wine bar later. Everybody'll be there. You know, a last night in town kind of thing."

"I'm going to pass."

"Oh, Lee! Come on, honey. You've got to get out a little." Ginny looked imploringly at Leanna in the mirror. "I know what you went through must have been awful, getting kidnapped and then that stay in the hospital, but you have to get back into things, you know?"

Leanna knew. She hadn't gotten back into anything, except dancing. She just couldn't seem to muster up the spirit for late-night gatherings or morning coffee, especially when everyone still had questions about what had happened to her.

The girls taken with her talked about how they'd been taken to a *souk* and almost immediately rescued by the local police. Leanna only said she'd been sold to a sultan and rescued by Americans who were in Baslaam on business.

All things considered, it wasn't exactly a lie.

"You're right, Gin, but I'm really beat tonight."

"Your poor foot, huh?"

"Uh-huh," Leanna said, because it was a lot easier to say that than to admit the truth.

All that stuff she'd told herself about infatuation was a lie.

She loved Cam. He was a brave man with no heart…and she would always love him.

The sooner she left Dallas, the better.

Cam was parked in his Porsche across from the hotel that housed the visiting *corps de ballet*.

He'd spent the evening pacing the antique kilim carpet in his darkened study. He couldn't stand still, couldn't sit still. Even his deep-breathing exercises had failed him.

When he realized he was checking his watch every thirty or forty seconds, he'd muttered an oath, grabbed his leather jacket and a couple of other things, and headed out the door.

He'd driven aimlessly for a while, taking a road that led out of the city, putting his foot to the floor when he reached a turn-off to an abandoned stretch of highway that was supposed to lead to the interstate but actually went nowhere. The road was known mostly to cops and street-racers. He'd let the Porsche fly until the car was running flat-out.

Then he'd eased off the gas and driven back to Dallas.

He had a good plan. Not flawless: no plan ever was. Luck, fate, kismet, whatever you wanted to call it, was always the unknown element. For all his careful organizing, he might still come up short.

Yeah, but the longer he sat here now, opposite the hotel, waiting for the P.I.'s call, the more he knew he had to do this.

Cam checked his watch again, the dial glowing an eerie green inside the dark car. "Come on," he muttered impatiently. "What's taking so freaking long?"

His gut was in knots. Excitement thrummed in his veins. Confronting a stranger named Leanna was all he could think about.

Leanna DeMarco. That was her name. Born in Boston, lived in a walk-up in Manhattan, danced ballet all her life, on tour with this company for the past six months.

The P.I. had phoned in late afternoon with all the pertinent information. Her name. Her background. The name of her hotel. Her room number.

He'd added that she shared her room with someone. For a second, the world had gone dark.

"Another dancer in the company," the P.I. said. "Virginia Adams. She and the subject appear to be good friends."

Cam had let out his breath. Another girl. Yeah. Okay—except, that might present a logistics problem.

"How good?" he said. "When the subject leaves the theater tonight, is she likely to be in the company of this Adams woman?"

She was, the P.I. said. The two dancers commonly traveled back and forth together.

Definitely a logistics problem, but not insoluble. Half an hour, and Cam had figured a way to deal with it. Rich Williams, a guy he'd played football with in college, was a features writer for the Dallas Register.

A phone call. A handful of good-natured "how's it goin'" and "remember when." Then, finally, a request.

"Lemme get this straight," Rich had said. "You want me to interview a dancer in a visiting ballet company?"

"Tonight, after the performance."

"Uh huh." Rich chuckled. "Seems to me I can recall the days you didn't need a setup like this to score points, buddy."

"Very funny," Cam had replied dryly.

"Well, you're in luck, man. I'm doing a piece on unusual jobs. Wouldn't hurt to add a dancer to the mix."

"Great. Take her out to supper. On me. Keep her busy for a couple of hours."

"Keep her...? You mean, the babe I'll be interviewing isn't the babe you've got your eye on?"

"She's her roommate," Cam said, telling the truth but tweaking it with a just-between-us-guys attitude he knew would work. "You know how it goes with women, Rich. They travel in pairs."

His friend had chuckled. "Gotcha."

Everything was set. So, why didn't the P.I. call? Cam glared at his cell. It was on, the battery was working and here in a nice, normal, civilized setting, all the little transmission bars were lit.

He was good to go, and he wanted this over with.

He knew who Salome was. Not just her name. Her. The woman. And he understood that she'd never been real.

Funny. One of the things he and his brothers used to

joke about was that most of the women they met couldn't be called "real."

"Take away the makeup," Matt would say, "the hair goop, the clothes and who the hell knows what you'd have left?"

"A naked babe," Alex would say solemnly, and they'd laugh.

Turned out it wasn't all that funny anymore.

What you had left, Cam thought grimly, without all the froufrou, was a woman who didn't exist. A woman who'd invented herself to suit the occasion.

A woman who'd claimed to love him.

What a lie.

Fantasy was her life. He'd seen that last night. The music. The sets. The costumes. Salome—make that Leanna—danced her way through life. She was a virginal princess one day and a sorceress the next.

She was like one of those toy ballerinas who came to life when you opened the lid of a music box.

And then, without warning, she'd found herself playing the role of a lifetime. A woman in jeopardy, with a man as different from the men in her world as night was from day.

Sleeping with him had been her walk on the wild side.

As for him… He'd been pulled straight into her fantasy. Either he wasn't as immune to adrenaline highs as he'd thought or his rush had come from taking a virgin.

The bottom line was, he'd had enough. It was time to put the experience behind him and the way to do that was to confront Salome. Damn it, confront Leanna.

He had to remember who she really was.

He'd considered waiting outside the theater but then

he'd realized she'd probably be surrounded by people. He didn't want this last scene in their little drama played before an audience.

Better to go to her hotel. Grab her as she came in. Except, the odds were good she'd still be with people. Friends—or maybe some guy. Maybe, with her innocence gone, she was busy exploring life.

She'd been good in bed. Incredible. For all he knew, she'd decided to enjoy herself.

Just because he lay awake nights, remembering how it had been, didn't mean she did. All the touching. The tasting. Sex that went from achingly tender to excitingly savage in a heartbeat.

Weeks had passed, and he hadn't forgotten.

Her whispers. The feel of her hand on him. The heat of her body as he sank into her. The way she trembled when she came.

Cam slammed his fist against the steering wheel. Why didn't the freaking phone ring?

In the end, he'd decided to catch her off guard. That meant doing this the way he knew best. Dress in dark clothes. Use the night as a cover. Slip into her room, wait for her, scare the crap out of her so she knew she couldn't make a fool of him and get away with it.

The cell phone rang. Cam let out a long, slow breath and flipped it open.

"I'm outside the theater," the P.I. said. "The subject's roommate is heading east with a man. Medium height. Light hair."

Cam nodded. Rich had done his job.

"And the subject?"

"Heading west, in the direction of her hotel."

A muscle knotted in Cam's jaw. "Is she alone?"

"Yes."

Perfect. Cam snapped the phone closed, tossed it on the passenger seat and settled in to wait.

CHAPTER THIRTEEN

THE hotel floor plans were on file at the city building department.

Cameron had studied them thoroughly. In late afternoon, he'd gone to the hotel and checked it out for himself.

Damned if he'd put a bunch of ballerinas in a place like this. He wasn't sure it even deserved being called a hotel.

The building was what he figured a Realtor would call a Victorian. It was really just an old and weary brick hulk. If it had seen better days, they were long past. This wasn't the best of neighborhoods, either. Not a bad one but certainly not the type the Chamber of Commerce would tout.

The idea of his Salome coming along this street at night, alone...

Except, she wasn't his Salome. She wasn't his anything. And if he had to give her credit for one thing, it was that she could take care of herself.

The building was big, though like many old structures it looked as if it had been added to as the city grew.

When he'd strolled inside earlier, he'd noticed that it was relatively well-cared for.

Not that its condition mattered.

His sole concern had been finding a way to get into Salome's room that didn't involve the hotel's front door or hers.

His reconnaissance had verified that an alley led to the rear of the building where fire escape stairs climbed the wall like the ossified bones of a dinosaur.

The window in Salome's room opened onto that fire escape.

Perfect for an intruder.

Perfect for him.

Something moved across the street. Cam took a pair of binoculars from the seat beside him. He'd considered a night-vision scope, but there was enough ambient light on a city street, even this one, for regular glasses to work.

He put the binoculars to his eyes, focused and felt his heart thud. Yes. It was Salome, walking quickly along the sidewalk. All that golden hair, that proud stride... It was her.

He watched her go up the steps to the front door of the hotel. Watched it shut behind her. Then he tossed aside the binoculars and slid a coiled length of rope inside his jacket. He zipped the jacket, stepped out of the Porsche and trotted across the street. A quick look to make sure nobody was coming, and then he went down the alley that led to the rear of the building. Stepped into the shadows, looked up to the third floor...

Saw the light come on in what he knew, from the P.I. and the plans, was her room.

Cam took a deep breath, threw his rope over the suspended fire escape ladder, and began to climb.

Leanna locked the door to her room behind her and watched her breath plume into the chilly air.

She always thought of Texas as a warm place. Silly, she knew. It was a huge state with different climates. This time of year, the weather in Dallas was cold.

It seemed even colder in this dingy room. She and Ginny had tried everything to get more heat out of the old-fashioned radiator. They'd jiggled the on-off handle, turned it up and turned it down. Ginny had finally whacked it with a shoe, but nothing worked. Give it a few minutes and you adjusted, although coming in from the cold each night remained a shock.

Surprisingly, there was no lack of hot water. A hot bath was fine for relaxing muscles that had taken a tough workout on stage, plus it took the chill out of your bones.

She shrugged off her jacket, went into the bathroom, turned on the water and began undressing. Naked, she swept her hair from her shoulders and pinned it on top of her head, then added bath oil to the steaming water.

The oil smelled of lavender, not flowers. That meant there was no reason it should make her think of Cam and yet, she was doing exactly that. Thinking of Cam. Of how it had felt to be in his arms as he stepped into a marble tub of scented water.

Leanna blinked.

The sooner she was out of this city, the better.

She shut the bathroom door, put a towel within easy reach and eased into the tub. Oh, yes. It felt wonderful to sit back and let the heat work its magic. There was nothing like a hot bath to soothe you at the end of a long and stressful day…

Nothing like a hot bath with your lover to turn a long, stressful day into the prelude to a long, wonderful night.

Stop it!

She was not going down that path again. All those weeks, telling herself Cam would call. That he'd come for her. Tell her that he did love her, that what he'd said that last day hadn't been true.

It had taken a long time before she'd faced reality, and she wasn't backing away from it now.

Cam wasn't going to come after her. He wasn't even going to telephone. And that was okay. He'd never made promises of forever. He hadn't fallen in love. She had…

And she still loved him.

Being here, where he lived and worked, knowing she had only to dial a number to hear his voice, was killing her. One call. Just one. She wouldn't have to say anything, except to his secretary, and then she could hear Cam's voice, add that memory to the others.

Suddenly the bath seemed cold. Leanna opened the drain, stepped from the tub, wrapped herself in a too thin, too small towel and opened the bathroom door…

On darkness.

Her heartbeat skittered.

How could that be? She'd left the room's single overhead light on. Even if the bulb had burned out, light should have been coming through the window. She was always careful to leave the window locked—the fire stairs outside were not reassuring—but she never drew the drab curtains until she and Ginny were ready to go to sleep. The room faced on a brick wall. Nobody could see in, but the light that filtered in from the alley, however faint, was welcome.

Could Ginny have come back already? Could she have drawn the curtains? Could the bulb in the ceiling light have gone out?

Could all that have happened at the same time?

"Ginny?" Leanna's whisper came out as half prayer, half question. "Gin? Is that—"

Something moved in the shadows. A figure. Tall. Broad-shouldered. A man. Leanna stumbled back in terror. *Oh God, oh God, oh God...*

The beam of a flashlight shone in her face. She gave a thin, high shriek, threw up a hand to shield her eyes.

"Hello, Salome," a rough voice said.

"Cameron?" Leanna went from terrified to thrilled in a heartbeat. He was here! He'd come for her after all. She whispered his name, started toward him...

And froze when the beam of light slid down her body, lingering on her breasts with slow insolence, rising again until it reached her face. Questions crowded out the joy she'd felt hearing his voice.

How had he gotten into the room? Why was he waiting in the dark?

"You don't seem very happy to see me."

Leanna jerked her head away from the cold yellow glare. "The light," she said. "I can't see."

The beam from the flashlight swung toward the floor. She blinked her eyes, trying to adjust to the dark. She could see Cam now, an inky blur against the charcoal shadows, moving slowly toward her.

Her heart began to race.

She'd longed to see him again and now he was here—but what did she know about him, really? He'd saved her life and made love to her. In the end, he'd broken her heart.

Aside from those things, he was a stranger. A hard and dangerous stranger. He'd worked for a government agency, he'd said, one so secret she wouldn't have recognized its initials.

Even the air crackled with menace.

He was inches from her now. She took a quick step back and her shoulders hit the wall.

"Don't," she said, and hated herself for the way the word wobbled.

"Don't what, Salome?" His words were soft as silk, but even silk could be deadly in the right hands. "I'm still waiting for you to tell me how glad you are to see me."

"I can't see you at all." That was better. She was shaking with fear but her voice was steady. "How did you get into my room?"

"Management needs to do something about that fire escape," he said lazily. "And that window lock wasn't worth a damn. How've you been, baby? Come to think of it, that's a foolish question. I know the answer. You've been busy."

His voice was harsh; he put an icy twist on that last word. She thought of the days she'd spent in the hospital but what would that matter to the man standing before her? Her Cameron had been tender. This one wouldn't know the meaning of the word.

"Cam." She swallowed past the lump in her throat. "Why—why did you break into my room? All you had to do, if you wanted to see me, was—"

"Why would I want to see you?" he said coldly. "We

had a good time, you and I, but it ended." The flashlight fell to the floor and he caught her by the shoulders, his hands hard against her flesh. "That's right, isn't it? What we had ended that day Asaad's men found us." She didn't answer; his grip on her tightened and he shook her. "Answer me, damn it. Isn't that the way it was?"

Tears blurred Leanna's eyes. "Why are you doing this?"

"Because I want answers."

"Cam. Please, let go. You're hurting me."

"You didn't say that the last time I touched you." She gasped as he tore the towel from her and pinned her to the wall with one hand banded around her throat. "Remember, Salome? *More,* you said. *More, Cameron.*" His voice roughened. "More of this."

His hand cupped her breast, his thumb feathered over her nipple. Leanna cried out in fear but her body, her traitorous body, began to melt under his remembered caresses.

"Don't," she said, "Cam, I beg you—"

"Good. Beg me. That's what I want from you tonight, Salome." Cam bent his head, caught her mouth with his, forced her lips apart. The taste of her shot through his blood. "Go on, damn you! Beg me. Tell me what you want."

His hand slid down her belly, cupped the soft gold curls that guarded the most intimate secrets of her body—secrets only he had known.

"This? Is this what you want from me?" He bent his head and tongued her nipple. She made a little sound that might have been despair or might have been pleasure. He didn't know, didn't care, didn't care…

Except, he did.

"Salome," he whispered, and his touch changed, his heart changed, his hand slipped from banding her throat to cupping her face. "Salome," he said again, and as he kissed her, he knew, with terrifying swiftness, that what he wanted from his Salome was to be with her for the rest of his life.

He loved her.

Loved her, with his heart, his mind, his soul.

It scared the hell out of him… But what scared him more was that she might not love him, too.

"Cameron," she said brokenly. "Please. Don't do this. What we had—what we had—"

"What did we have, Salome?"

"You—you said it yourself. It was a fantasy. The danger. The excitement—"

"Is that all it was?"

She didn't answer. Her eyes slid from his and he prayed it was because she loved him.

"Salome. Remember what I said in the desert? I told you to stop thinking." He framed her face with his hands. "That's what I want you to do now, sweetheart. Don't think. Just feel—and tell me what's in your heart." He took a deep breath. "Tell me that you love me, Leanna." His voice roughened. "Tell me you love me as much as I love you."

She stared at him in silence. Then, when he'd almost given up hope, she choked out a sound halfway between a sob and laughter.

"Cameron," she said. "Oh, Cameron, my beloved."

The world, his anger, the disillusionment Cam had carried with him most of his life, were all swept away. He caught Leanna to him and kissed her.

She tasted as she had in his dreams, sweet as honey, rich as cream. Her tears, under the sweep of his thumbs, were warm as summer rain. And when she sighed his name, he knew he would forgive her for not coming to him, that he would forgive her for anything as long as he never lost her again.

"Salome," he whispered.

He lifted her into his arms, his mouth on hers, his tongue between her lips, and carried her the few feet to the bed. He lay her down slowly, still kissing her, torn between wanting the kiss to go on forever and the need to pull off his clothes, bury himself inside her and make her his again.

Leanna dug her hands into his hair. "Don't leave me," she begged. "Cameron, don't ever leave me again."

"Never," he said fiercely.

He took her hands and kissed them, bent to her and nipped her throat, kissed his way to her breasts, exulting in the richness of her scent as he sucked the beaded tips into his mouth. When she cried out in pleasure, Cam tore off his jacket, his shirt, then scooped her tightly against him, groaning aloud at the feel of her skin on his.

"Tell me you've missed me," he demanded. "Tell me you've dreamed about me doing this."

"Yes," Leanna sobbed, "yes, yes! I've missed you. I've dreamed about you. Cam. Come inside me. Please, I want you inside me. I need to feel you. I need—"

She arched against him as he slid his hand between her thighs. She was wet and hot, for him. Only for him, he knew, and then he couldn't wait, couldn't wait, could only unzip his fly, spread his hands beneath her, lift her to him, drive deep inside her...

Her scream of completion rose into the night. She

locked her arms around his neck and rose up to him, her body convulsing around his, her fingernails scoring his back. Cam rode the wave of ecstasy with her, letting the first delicate contraction of her womb sweep him toward the edge of sanity.

He crushed her mouth with his, bit into the tender flesh, tasted blood—hers or his, he didn't know, didn't care—as she sucked his tongue into her mouth.

Sobbing his name, Salome collapsed against the pillows.

Cam flung back his head, cried out, and flew with her into paradise.

Leanna had read that the French sometimes referred to orgasm as *le petit mort*. The little death. The phrase had seemed elegant but impossible.

Now, she knew the truth of it.

Surely she had died of ecstasy in her lover's arms.

Long seconds passed. Somehow, she dragged breath into her lungs. Cam rolled onto his side with her still tightly held in his embrace.

"My Salome," he said softly, pressing a kiss to her closed eyelids.

His Salome. Her heart swelled at the sound of the name that belonged only to the two of them.

"Cam," she said, just as softly. She cupped her hand around his jaw, felt the rough silk of his end-of-day stubble, and met his lips in a long, slow kiss. "I'm so glad you're all right."

"I'm very all right," he said, laughing softly.

She smiled. "Yes. Oh, yes, you are. But I meant, I'm so glad you—you—"

"You're glad I what, sweetheart?"

"Lived," she said, her voice breaking.

Was it her imagination, or did he pull away just a little?

"Yeah," he said, and cleared his throat. "Well, me, too." A second slipped by. He cleared his throat again. "If it mattered to you—if it did, how come you never—how come you never—"

"Never what?"

"Never called," he said, trying not to sound the way he felt, like a kid who'd lost everything because, damn it, without her, he *had* lost everything. He rose up on his elbow and looked down into her shadowed face. "You didn't come to me, Salome," he said roughly. "And, God, I wanted you. I longed for you. But you didn't—"

"I called," Leanna said, putting her hand over his mouth to stop the flow of words. "Every day. Every night. All the time you were in the hospital."

Cam stared at her. "You did?"

"I almost went out of my mind, not being with you. Even after—after what you'd said, that you didn't love me—"

"I was lying, sweetheart. To you and to myself. I'd have said anything to keep you in that room." He kissed her, his mouth moving gently on hers. "And I was afraid to admit that I loved you."

Leanna closed her eyes, then opened them again. "I thought—I believed—"

"Is that why you didn't come to me all those weeks in the hospital?"

"I couldn't come." She hesitated. "I was sick, Cam."

"Sick?" He sat up, gathering her against him. She

could feel the swift acceleration of his heart. "What happened? Why didn't you let me know?"

"An infection, in my foot. I couldn't let you know. I mean, at first I was too ill. And then, when I was better…" A sob burst from her throat. "I knew you didn't want me."

He kissed her, and she could almost feel the love flowing from his heart to hers.

"I wanted you every moment, Salome. Those endless weeks in the hospital, all the ones since… You were all I could think about."

"Then—then why…" Tears rose in her eyes. "When I knew you were out of the hospital, I let myself begin to hope. Each time the phone rang, each time the mail came— Someone would knock at the door and my heart would say, *It's him, it's Cameron, he's come.* And—and you never…"

She began to weep. Cam brushed his lips over hers again and again, until her mouth softened and clung to his.

"Salome," he said softly, "my sweet Salome. I couldn't come to you, baby. You were my golden dancer. My Salome. My forever love." He gave a ragged laugh. "Only one problem, sweetheart. I didn't know your name."

Leanna drew back in his embrace and stared at him. "What?"

"Your real name. I didn't know it. That's why I didn't come to you. I couldn't find you. I flew to Dubai. I hired a detective. I did everything I could think of—" he grinned "—including drive my brothers crazy." His smile faded. "And then, when I'd all but given up hope, my old man talked me into going to a performance at—"

"The Music Hall! I knew you were there! I felt it. Oh, Cam—"

Cam kissed her, long and sweetly. "I'm sorry if I frightened you tonight."

"You thrilled me. When I realized it was you—"

"Salome. I mean, Leanna—"

"No." She kissed him, her mouth curving against his. "Salome," she whispered. "I like that much better."

Cam rolled her beneath him. "I'm never going to lose you again."

That won him another kiss. "I won't let you."

"I'll just have to keep you where I can see you." His eyes darkened. He bent to her and kissed her throat. "In bed, with me."

"Mmm."

"Any objections?"

"Mmm," Leanna said again, and gently moved her hips.

"Of course," he said, his voice thick. "I can think of one other way."

"Yes?"

"Salome. My beloved dancer, will you marry me?"

Leanna gave him her answer with a kiss.

HARLEQUIN®
Presents

**The world's bestselling romance series...
The series that brings you your favorite authors,
month after month:**

Helen Bianchin...Emma Darcy
Lynne Graham...Penny Jordan
Miranda Lee...Sandra Marton
Anne Mather...Carole Mortimer
Susan Napier...Michelle Reid

and many more uniquely talented authors!

Wealthy, powerful, gorgeous men...
Women who have feelings just like your own...
The stories you love, set in exotic, glamorous locations...

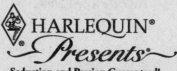

HARLEQUIN®
Presents

Seduction and Passion Guaranteed!

HPDIR104